KORMA, KHEER AND KISMET

KORMA, KHEER AND KISMET

Five Seasons in Old Delhi

Pamela Timms

ALEPH

ALEPH

ALEPH BOOK COMPANY
An independent publishing firm
promoted by *Rupa Publications India*

Published in India in 2014 by
Aleph Book Company
7/16 Ansari Road, Daryaganj
New Delhi 110002

Copyright © Pamela Timms 2014

Photographs Copyright © Pamela Timms

All rights reserved.

No part of this publication may be reproduced, transmitted, or stored in a retrieval system, in any form or by any means, without permission in writing from Aleph Book Company.

ISBN: 978-93-82277-14-9

3 5 7 9 10 8 6 4 2

Printed and bound in India by Replika Press Pvt. Ltd.

For sale in the Indian subcontinent only.

This book is sold subject to the condition that it shall not, by way of trade or otherwise, be lent, resold, hired out, or otherwise circulated without the publisher's prior consent in any form of binding or cover other than that in which it is published.

*To Dean, Charlie, Georgia and Fergus—
without you there would have been no adventures.*

*And for my mother,
who taught me the value of eating well.*

Contents

Author's Note   *ix*
List of Recipes   *xi*

1. The Mutton Korma Mysteries   1
2. From Irn-Bru to Ecrevisses   20
3. A Refuge in Old Delhi   32
4. Independence Day in Sadar Bazaar   45
5. Homesick Restaurants   61
6. Sheher   79
7. Shakarkandi in Ballimaran   90
8. Fasting and Feasting   105
9. Kheer and Kismet   122
10. Mughal Breakfasts and Jalebi Brunches   133
11. God's Own Street Food   146
12. At Home in Old Delhi   158

Acknowledgements   167

Author's Note

Although this book revolves around the events of a particular year, it is also the product of the many more I have spent exploring and eating my way round Old Delhi. Of the almost ten years I have lived in Delhi, it is the times I have spent in the old city which have been my happiest; it is an area that never fails to enchant and amaze me. I did not set out to write the definitive guide to every cart and shack, and I know some readers will be disappointed not to find their own favourites here. To them I can only say that this is an account of my five seasons in Old Delhi, a celebration of both the food that means most to me and the extraordinary people I've met along the way.

List of Recipes

Goggia Uncle's 'Ashok and Ashok' Mutton Korma	17
Roast Chicken with Pasta and Tomatoes	30
Baba Singh's Amritsari Kulcha	42
Aloo Tikki	59
Pandit Kuremal's Kulfi	72
Kuremal's Falsa Kulfi	73
Sita Ram Diwan Chand's Chana Bhatura	74
Mr Naseem's Sheer Khurma	88
Roasted Sweet Potato or Shakarkandi	103
Meena Pimplapure's Chirote	119
Bade Mian's Kheer	132
Jalebis	144
Daulat Ki Chaat	155
Kamlesh Arora's Chana Puri and Sooji Halwa	165

ONE

The Mutton Korma Mysteries

Every morning the newspapers screamed what we already knew—'No Respite for Delhi-ites from Harsh Summer Sun', 'Delhi Sweats it Out', 'Power Cuts Worsen in Delhi Summer'—and we wilted a little bit more. By the end of April, for most of the day, the blazing, dusty streets of our South Delhi neighbourhood were deserted—the only movement an occasional creaking bicycle and slow, yellow snow falling from the laburnum trees. Even the otherwise perennially cheerful and bustling sari-clad fruit sellers sat slumped in the shade with their baskets of mangoes, their fruit turning to mush in front of them. We only saw our neighbours in the early morning when they emerged briefly from shuttered and shaded houses to buy vegetables; they seemed to spend the rest of their time compiling data from meteorological bulletins, which they would share the following day. 'No relief from heat,' said one, taking a seasonal break from advising me on whether to buy aubergine or okra. 'Monsoon is playing truant.'

The great fin-de-siècle Delhi writer Ahmed Ali once described the Delhi summer as the season of 'unending noon'. Now it's a time of endless Facebook screenshots of temperatures heading towards fifty degrees centigrade and accompanying descriptions of physical and mental meltdown. Surprisingly, despite this annual thesaurus of scorch, no one ever quite nails the sheer life-sapping feeling of being trapped inside a tandoor for three months of the year.

We tried to beat the heat by getting up while it was still dark, at about the same time as the early morning call to prayer from the mosque on the corner, and by 6 a.m. we were walking our dogs in Lodhi Gardens. Many had the same idea—even at that hour the park's walking track resembled the Outer Ring Road as hundreds snatched a few moments outside before the daytime air-conditioned purdah. Senior civil servants, trailed by hapless flunkies and their chorus of 'haan ji, sir ji', marched alongside Lycra-clad runners and ladies in flapping kurtas; youngsters were making the most of the school holidays, playing cricket and football; and the yoga class in the rose garden was in full swing. Near the Bara Gumbad, servants were laying out tablecloths and unpacking picnic hampers from their bicycles for the group of distinguished elderly gentlemen that meets every morning to put the world to rights over breakfast. The park dogs kept a lazy eye on proceedings from the cooling pits they'd dug for themselves, while the flaming tops of the gulmohar trees forecast the discomfort of the day ahead.

One morning we bumped into Mr Lal, a canine-friendly senior civil servant who plies our dogs with treats and is always happy to spend a few moments discussing the weather. The onset of summer seemed to have made him philosophical. The hot weather, he told us, despite driving us to the brink of insanity, was actually a good thing. 'It develops certain characteristics,' he said. With that he plugged himself back into his iPod and power-walked off, leaving us to wonder what he meant—probably fortitude, determination and a backbone as upright as his own. I thought

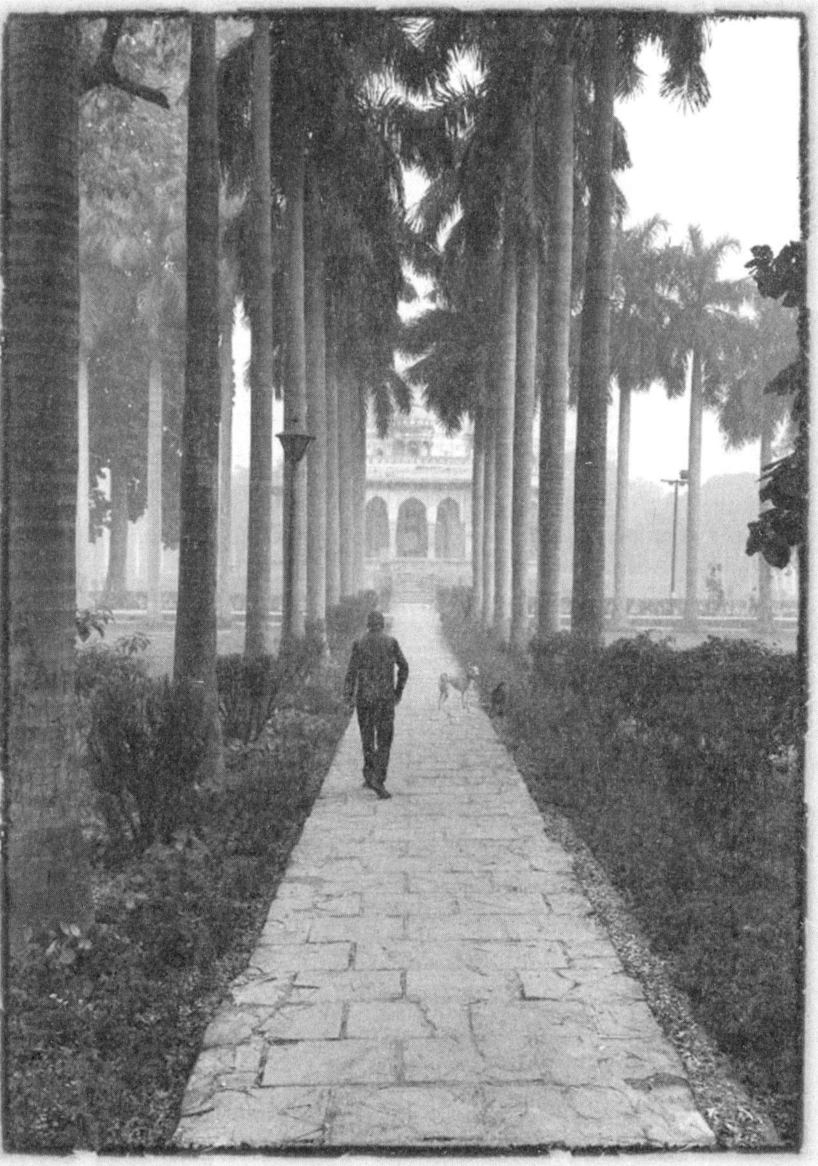

about Mr Lal's words one Sunday a few weeks later when I decided the characteristics the summer had developed in me were the first signs of madness.

I was sitting in a tiny meat shop in Sadar Bazaar—one of the city's least photogenic spots—as dust, dirt, flies and diesel fumes swarmed in from the street outside and stagnant, fetid air trapped every passing smell, fragrant and foul. The butcher, Mohammed Gulrez Qureshi, was perched on top of the shop's counter, cross-legged behind a huge slice of tree trunk. Next to him sat a young apprentice on a tomb-sized slab of marble from which hung a fluffy tail, a defiantly lively tuft still attached to the rear end of its recently skinned and dismembered owner. Both of them seemed oblivious to the searing heat, which was testing even the marble's resolve. The shop was about the size of a large cupboard into which had been crammed, apart from the two butchers, half a dozen fresh goat carcasses, an ancient set of scales and a shelf of ready-made masalas. In front of the counter, almost nose to tail with the meat, and giving the impression of an audience waiting for a performance to begin, sat my husband, Dean, two men I had just met—Mr Goggia and his nephew, Anuj—and I.

Qureshi looked over to his customers, quietly awaiting instruction. Old Mr Goggia muttered a few barely audible words. The butcher selected a shoulder and rack of mutton, placed it in the centre of the tree-trunk chopping board, slowly sharpened his well-worn cleaver, then reduced the whole lot to a neat pile of pot-ready chunks. With a few more samurai blows he created a mound of minced meat, then slid it all into a plastic bag and handed it down. Mr Goggia took the bag and started to walk towards the door but I was still staring at Qureshi's blade as if it were the Holy Grail, jotting down the exact size of the pieces of meat, scrutinizing the tree trunk, grooved and gashed by generations of use, even assessing the precise angle at which blade met flesh.

What was I doing in Mr Qureshi's shop that day, obsessing over pieces of mutton with assorted men named Goggia and a husband denied his Sunday lie-in and air-conditioned brunch? The short answer is that I was researching a street food dish I had eaten a few months earlier. The long one begins with a rickshaw ride through Old Delhi in 2010.

I had arrived in Khari Baoli, Asia's largest spice market, in time to watch the start of one of the world's greatest pieces of street theatre. The flower sellers, as always, opened the show, slashing open their vast sacks and letting a tricolour of marigold, jasmine and rose tumble out on to the street. Then, as the spice vendors' shutters flew up and hundreds of small pyramids of dried fruit, nuts and spices appeared, a cast of thousands began to emerge. An army of sweepers cleared mountains of debris from the previous day and threw up clouds of dust with their twiggy brooms while chai wallahs crouched over their stoves, hurrying to make the spicy brew that would get the market moving. Portly spice merchants started to stroll in from their homes in the suburbs, tended to their pujas, garlanded portraits of their ancestors and prayed fervently for a good day's trading. Scrawny porters dragged aching limbs from sleep. The lucky ones were curled up on the handcarts that served as both home and workplace; the less fortunate were waking up on the pavement or the roof of Gadodia Market. Most wore long shirts and lungis, with checked scarves flung over their shoulders, ready to wipe away sweat and cushion heavy loads. As the tea slowly worked its magic and traders turned their attention to the day's business, the porters loaded up their carts or heads with sacks and boxes. For the rest of the day, they would race back and forth, delivering goods to shops, trucks and railway stations, oblivious to anyone who got in their way. (A common souvenir of a trip to

Old Delhi is a set of bruises from collisions with market porters.) Later, when the work had run out or complete exhaustion taken over, they would wash themselves and their clothes at standpipes, then eat their only meal—for most of the day they are powered by gutkha—and perhaps smoke a bidi, the tiny hand-rolled fast track to emphysema and lung cancer. On a good day there might be a card game or a few swigs of cheap rum.

For a while I was mesmerized by the magnificent mayhem of the spice market—buyers adopting an air of indifference as they assessed and haggled over turmeric, cardamom, pepper, nuts, fruit and tea; wily traders driving hard bargains, one hand always on their giant metal cash boxes; the constant coughing of traders, porters, sweepers, chai wallahs and tourists from the fumes of a thousand sacks of dried red chillies until, by mid-morning, the market was a frazzled, hacking, teeming gridlock. But I had to tear myself away. I had heard that one of Old Delhi's finest plates of food was to be found in the area just beyond the spice market in Sadar Bazaar.

The boundary between the two areas was marked by a slight incline where a long tailback of cycle rickshaws, market porters, bullock carts and shoppers on foot had brought the road to a standstill. Suddenly, the spectacular displays of spices gave way to the more prosaic commerce of plastic toys from China, counterfeit perfumes, garish wedding supplies and what looked like second-hand dentures. Thousands of locals, as well as traders from all over northern India, were jammed into the warren of streets, hell-bent on nailing the best prices on cheap crockery, glass, steel, kitchenware, ironmongery, election banners, stationery and fireworks. Despite the merciless heat, Rahul, my rickshaw driver, powered through the nursery slopes of Sadar Bazaar, dismissing my offers to dismount and only conceded defeat when we reached our final destination, where he sheepishly asked me to walk the last few yards.

Apart from being unusually steep, Subhas Chowk turned out to be a relatively quiet, nondescript street. There was a sweet shop doing a brisk trade in chhole bhature and a vendor firing up his jalebi pan, but nothing to suggest I was in the presence of culinary greatness. Heading upwards, I dodged a fast-flowing stream of waste near a tea stall, where a young boy was crouching over the gutter, scraping steel plates and rinsing them in a plastic tub of murky water. It was a few minutes before I noticed a faded, grimy sign—'Ashok and Ashok Meat Dhaba', although the shop itself was sealed with a battered steel shutter. A passing local told me I was early, the shop didn't open till 1 p.m., so I ordered a cup of sweet chai from the stall and found a ledge to sit it out.

Groups of hungry-looking men started to arrive, but nearly an hour later there was still no sign of life. Soon, about thirty men, a macho-looking bunch with Bollywood shades and slicked-back hair, were hovering around the shop looking at watches and wondering aloud about the delay. Most of the men seemed to be regulars—one told me that he and his team of travelling salesmen had compiled a list of the best places to eat all over India. 'Shokkys',' he said, 'is definitely in the top five. We always come here for Diwali lunch.' He couldn't quite put into words why they were so devoted to the food we were all waiting for—Ashok and Ashok's korma—but the words 'tender', 'rich', 'spicy' and 'ghee' were uttered with a faraway look in his eyes.

Just as it seemed the good-natured banter and anticipation could topple over into unrest and anarchy, a skinny young man hauled out two grimy trestle tables, set them on the edge of the foul-looking gutter and gave them a cursory wipe with a blackened rag. Then a well-built surly, stubbly man, oblivious to the mounting tension, made his way through the crowd. First, he released the steel shutter to reveal a high counter and a large, faded portrait of two unsmiling thickset men who looked as if they were keeping a beady eye on proceedings. He then snapped on a cassette player and a further agonizing few minutes passed as we waited for him to perform his puja. Finally, he turned and gave a sign. From nowhere, it seemed, large metal pots were borne in trailing clouds of ghee and spice. The waiters started to throw metal plates of sliced onion and lemon down on to the tables, and we all prepared to eat. But the agony was still far from over. A murmur rippled through the crowd that the rotis weren't ready and all eyes turned accusingly to the young man a little further up the street, hurriedly slapping discs of dough into a tandoor. Shoulders drooped—Shokkys' korma is nothing, I was told, nothing, without bread to ensure no drop of the precious gravy goes un-mopped. Bottles of Thums Up were ordered, mobile phones fiddled with, mouths watered, fingers tapped. 'To know how to eat well,' these men didn't need Brillat-Savarin to tell them, 'one must first know how to wait.'

A nervy silence gripped the diners; then at last the rotis were ready and plates of korma were unceremoniously slapped down in front of us. Juicy pieces of mutton shimmered in a lake of deep mahogany sauce—so far removed from the anaemic, gloopy, bland concoctions that go by the same name in British curry houses as to be an entirely different species. Armed with pieces of hot, crisp, coriander-laced rotis, we all dived in. Some immediately started chewing on the bones but most of us made straight for the gravy. The first taste was an eye-watering blast of chilli heat that had me spluttering and reaching for the water bottle. This was quickly followed by layers of more nuanced, elusive ingredients—'Up to thirty different spices,' one of my dining companions assured me between mouthfuls—in a devilish pact with ghee. The meat itself had been cooked long and slow, and fell away easily from the bone at a nudge from the bread. For the few minutes it took us to devour our korma, no one uttered a word, and we paused only to signal to the waiters when more rotis were required. Too soon, we were again staring at empty plates, this time with no hope of a refill. The day's korma was already sold out.

As soon as I had resigned myself to the fact that there would be no seconds, I tried to talk to the owners. I wanted a few quotes for my blog to accompany a fulsome description of the meal I had just eaten. I had started the blog a few months earlier as a way of recording my food adventures in India and had generally found vendors happy to chat and had even managed to prise some recipes from them. But at Ashok and Ashok I couldn't even catch the surly one's eye. He simply pretended he hadn't heard my questions and held out his hand for payment.

I walked back down the street to console myself with jalebis, knowing no more about Ashok and Ashok and their mutton korma than when I arrived. But what I had seen contradicted everything I thought I knew about great eating experiences. First of all, Ashok and Ashok's approach to hygiene is enough to give a health and safety inspector nightmares. The ambience and décor is what might be tactfully described as 'no-frills'—in fact, things would need to improve considerably to reach 'no-frills'. The front of house is at the rude end of the efficiency/offensive spectrum and there's an interminable wait for the food. The menu is extremely limited—in fact there are only two dishes on offer—biryani and korma (chicken every day, mutton on Wednesday and Saturday), both of which are, I had gathered, finished within an hour of opening. And yet, those two dishes, I discovered, were heart-stoppingly good—possibly literally, given the amount of ghee involved. It was food to crave and get misty-eyed over; food to brave filthy backstreets and a searing Delhi summer for.

The reluctance of the 'Shokkys' to tell me anything about their history or recipe was disappointing. Puzzling too, because I was already starting to sense that Old Delhi's street food vendors, like great restaurateurs the world over, understand the importance of talking up a colourful backstory, the unique narrative that enhances a restaurant's reputation, mystique and custom. Most of the vendors I met had shared, at the very least, eventful family histories involving heroic ancestral migration, often at the time of India's Partition, and hinted at secret family recipes more closely guarded than the formula for Coca-Cola.

Over the next few months, I was a regular at Ashok and Ashok but never managed to get a word out of the owners. It was only when I started to ask around that I began to understand why they might be uncharacteristically tight-lipped. Gradually, I discovered the shop had no shortage of colourful history, in fact there were many versions of their story—none of which they seemed to want the world to know about.

I started with some online research. What I found was

intriguing—as well as salivating reviews of Ashok and Ashok's food, there was the occasional reference to 'hoodlums' and 'toughies'. One newspaper food columnist, Rahul Verma, who claimed to have known the shop's founders, was more explicit. '[They] ran one of the best dhabas in Delhi that I have ever been to,' he wrote. 'The friends, both called Ashok, were engaged in some nefarious deals in the daytime, and in the evening, when they gathered with their booty, they would pool in their money, buy some meat and make the most delicious mutton dish of all time. It was such a hit with their friends and neighbours that they gave up their old ways and became professional cooks. And people from far and wide [...] used to go there for their meat dish. The two friends are no more but their sons and nephews are carrying on with the lip-smacking legacy of "desi ghee ka meat".'* If this were true, I thought, the current owners were probably happy to let their food do the talking rather than the family history.

The oracle of our times, Twitter, was uncharacteristically quiet on the matter but @harpritbhatia, who works near Ashok and Ashok in the Bara Hindu Rao area, also offered a similar account, in 140 character snatches, of the shop's history:

@harpritbhatia: I used to & still have an office [at] Sadar. My suppliers were based around Bara [Hindu Rao], they told me the story

@harpritbhatia: These guys (Ashoks) used to operate in Bara Hindu Rao area. Petty thieves turned musclemen

@harpritbhatia: Story: In burning hot summers, after ripping off/hitting some people, they were coming back. Saw some Sikhs distributing free water

@harpritbhatia: Upon asking why, a local elder told them,

---
*Rahul Verma, *The Telegraph*, 29 April 2012

more joy in sharing with the fellow people, rather than looting from them, & they changed

@harpritbhatia: yes, it's part of the old folklore. A saintly old man gave them a gentle lesson and they changed overnight

I loved the idea of an epiphany on the road to food heaven and it certainly seemed to confirm there was something in the Ashoks' background which might explain the surly demeanour of the proprietor at the shop and his unwillingness to chat.

Months passed, another summer stormed in, then one day, while researching a newspaper story on something entirely unrelated to mutton korma, Dean was chatting with a former Sadar Bazaar resident named Anuj Goggia. In a bid to steer the conversation away from whichever controversial issue they were discussing, Dean mentioned our love of Ashok and Ashok's food and that I was trying to find out a bit more about the family and their recipes. 'Hah!' said Goggia. 'My family's from Subhas Chowk, right next to Shokkys. Come over on Sunday, meet my uncle, he knew the Ashoks well. In fact, he can show your wife how to make their mutton korma.'

Up to that point, our blistering summer weekends had revolved around air-conditioned cinemas or friends with swimming pools but that Sunday found Dean and I, in the middle of the day, on the blistering hot pavement outside a closed Ashok and Ashok, where we were joined by a couple of dusty goats chewing on bits of paper. Eventually, Anuj arrived with his uncle, a small, taciturn man in his sixties with bright orange hennaed hair who looked as if he might still give his nephew a clip round the ear if he answered back. Goggia Uncle barely acknowledged us before speeding off down the hill, leaving Anuj to explain that before we could watch the korma being made we had to get the meat. As we trailed after Goggia Uncle to the butchers' colony a few streets away, there was something in his manner that made me think I might have to prove myself by first slaughtering a goat or at the very least watch one being slaughtered. I was immensely relieved when he led us into a shop where there was plenty of evidence the slaughtering had already taken place. Anuj explained that the family have always bought their meat from the Qureshis, a family of butchers who have been in Qasab Pura for over sixty years, because they are confident the animals have been grass-fed and jhatka-slaughtered in accordance with Hindu tradition. Goggia Uncle muttered something, one of the few utterances he would make all day, and the butcher got to work. The four of us sat patiently on the bench opposite and I tried to write down anything that might help me demystify the wonder of Ashok and Ashok's mutton korma... 'Jhatka method,' I scribbled. 'Grass-fed...chopping board made from tree trunk...'

As we slogged back up the hill to the Goggias' house, in temperatures in the mid-forties centigrade, laden with plastic bags of freshly cut mutton, I tried to engage Goggia Uncle in conversation. I quickly realized he wasn't one for small talk, or in fact any kind of talk—all my questions about the Ashoks, hoodlums, even the weather, were either ignored or met with an exasperated frown. We continued in silence for a while, dodging street cricket matches and groups of men playing cards on the pavement. I had almost resigned myself to a wasted trip when Goggia Uncle muttered something under his breath. Anuj looked genuinely startled. 'He says that he was the one who taught the two Ashoks how to make the korma.' There was a bit more muttering as I processed what we'd just heard, then Anuj announced, 'He says Ashok and Ashok won their restaurant in a card game, but those guys had no idea how to cook anything so they approached my uncle. He taught them everything they knew.' Despite my spluttering and excitable requests for clarification, Goggia Uncle's lips were sealed. I trailed after him hoping for more detail, but it seemed he had said all he was going to on the matter. But I was starting to believe that the dish I was about to watch being prepared might be the original version of the one I had eaten and loved months before.

We climbed the narrow, almost vertical, dark stone stairs to the Goggias' home and a crack of light appeared to guide us to a few rooms arranged along the edge of the roof. Like thousands of others, the Goggias left Pakistan at the time of Partition in 1947 and have lived in the barsati of an increasingly dilapidated tenement building in Sadar Bazaar ever since. Gradually, as with many of the area's families, most of the younger generation—including nephew Anuj—have now moved out, leaving a handful of ageing aunts and uncles to see out their days in the old family home.

Anuj ushered us into the main living area, a small room where layers of blue and green paintwork looped backwards and forwards over the decades and a high, corniced ceiling and colonial verandah-style chairs suggested earlier, grander times. The room was open on both sides to catch any passing breeze. On one side, shutters gave on to a small balcony where a mound of grain and crumbs encouraged pigeons to stop and carry the family's prayers up to heaven. On the other, a tiny room crammed with tables, chairs, beds and fridges, piles of bedding, clothes and the last few remaining Goggia family members opened out on to the roof. On that sweltering May day, though, breeze was in short supply and we had to make do with an ancient, creaking ceiling fan to keep the air moving. Unfortunately it seemed to be merely distributing the blistering dry heat more evenly, desiccating lips and searing eyeballs and making us feel as if we were being baked in a giant fan-assisted oven.

Word had gone out that Goggia Uncle was cooking korma, and friends and family started to arrive. One of Anuj's friends had driven across town, leaving his wife at home with their newborn baby. 'Goggia Uncle's mutton is more important,' he said. The men cracked open some beers and started to reminisce about the good times and great meals they'd shared in the house. Anuj told us that although his wing of the family moved away from Sadar Bazaar in 1966, all of his childhood summer holidays and festivals were spent here, and Goggia Uncle's korma was always made for special celebrations. As the beer and whisky started to flow, and famished expectation grew, I slipped out to watch the cook at work.

Goggia Uncle's kitchen was no more than a tiny dark cupboard with barely enough room for one person and a two-burner stove. Cooking utensils and plastic jars of staples and spices formed a collage over every inch of the crumbling plastered walls. The preparation of ingredients had extended to the roof where Goggia Auntie and a young niece were chopping onion, garlic and ginger. Inside the cubbyhole, with his back to everything, Goggia Uncle devoted himself to the alchemy of spice. There was no question of me being in the kitchen at the same time so I loitered awkwardly outside, rushing to peer over his shoulder every time a new ingredient was added, again scribbling down every detail. 'Brown onions very well...two heaped teaspoons garam masala... stir constantly.' He politely confirmed the list of ingredients and gave me a hint of a wry smile when I said I'd heard there were around thirty different spices in Ashok and Ashok's korma. But when I tried to press him on precise quantities and technique, he answered with a frowning 'aisa hi hai' and returned to stirring his pot, leaving me to jot down estimates in my notebook. One tip he did share is the practice of taking along your own flavourings to the butcher to be blended with the minced meat; for the bespoke Goggia mix, green chilli, ginger and fresh coriander are added, although in what proportions, Uncle wasn't saying. I noted too, that like the Ashok and Ashok version, a healthy dollop of ghee is added but said I was surprised there were no ground nuts in the recipe. 'No nuts,' said Goggia Uncle, definitively. Eventually, he explained that the gravy is thickened instead with the minced mutton. 'In fact,' he said, with a curl of the lip, 'these days Ashok and Ashok are adding much more of keema and ghee to eke out cheaper cuts of meat.'

For two hours we were tormented by rich spicy smells coming from Goggia Uncle's kitchen, and by the time the food was ready, the men had finished the whisky and beer and korma fever had turned rowdy. When Goggia Auntie finally filled up our plates, I paused a second longer than everyone else; just long enough to take in the strong physical resemblance to the Ashok and Ashok version, the rich dark brown gravy glistening with ghee, the sauce begging to be mopped, bones to be gnawed clean. The silence that descended when we started to eat was also identical, the only sounds the creak of the fan, the licking of fingers and smacking of lips. We all ate as if it were our last meal—silent, greedy and thankful.

I left Sadar Bazaar that summer Sunday in 2011 on the verge of heat stroke and ready for our annual few weeks' chilly respite in Scotland. But I was also well-fed and elated, with a notebook full of recipes and amusing anecdotes. I would never know whether I'd just eaten the original Ashok and Ashok mutton korma—though they tasted identical—but I was already certain that my afternoon in Sadar Bazaar had given me a lot more than a delicious meal. By taking me into his home and letting me watch him cook, Goggia Uncle had officially opened my year of eating in Old Delhi.

GOGGIA UNCLE'S 'ASHOK AND ASHOK' MUTTON KORMA

SERVES 6-8

The mutton korma I enjoyed at the Goggias' home that day was almost identical to the Ashok and Ashok one. However, despite noting down every ingredient added and movement made, when I tried to replicate the dish, mine was slightly different, very similar in flavour but with a less smooth texture. I think the secret must be in Mohammed Qureshi's knife skills—for the smoothest, silkiest korma, the keema needs to be very finely minced.

INGREDIENTS

    6 tbsp ghee

    2 onions, peeled and grated

    4 thumb-sized pieces of ginger, peeled and grated

    6 garlic cloves, grated

    1 tbsp garam masala

    1 brown cardamom

    5 green cardamoms

    6 cloves

    10 black peppercorns

    500 gms minced mutton (make sure the meat is as finely minced as possible)

    1.5 kg small pieces of mixed shoulder and rack of mutton

    2 tsp turmeric

    1 heaped tsp red chilli powder

    2 tsp salt

    10 medium-sized tomatoes, skinned, seeds removed and finely chopped

    A few slices of ginger and coriander to garnish

METHOD

Melt the ghee in a large pan. Add the onions, ginger and garlic and cook until well browned, 10-15 minutes. Add the garam masala, brown and green cardamoms, cloves and peppercorns and stir well. Add the minced mutton and mutton pieces, coating well with the spices. Stir in the turmeric, chilli powder and salt, then cook on a low heat for about 20 minutes until everything is well browned.

Add the chopped tomatoes and enough water to cover the meat then simmer gently for 1-1½ hours till the gravy is thick and glossy. Check seasoning and add more salt or chilli if required. Garnish with slivers of chopped ginger and fresh coriander and serve with roti.

CORIANDER AND CHILLI ROTI

MAKES 12

The roti served at Ashok and Ashok is seared in a tandoor. This recipe is an easy way of achieving a similar bread at home.

INGREDIENTS

- 300 gms wholemeal flour (atta)
- 1 tsp baking powder
- 300 gms plain yogurt
- 3 small green chillies, finely chopped
- A large handful of fresh coriander, finely chopped
- Ghee for frying

METHOD

Mix together the flour, baking powder, yogurt, chillies and

coriander. Knead for a few minutes to form a smooth, firm dough. Wrap in cling film and rest in the fridge for at least an hour.

When you're ready to serve the roti, divide the dough into twelve pieces. Roll each piece into a ball then roll out as thinly as possible—about 2 mm thick. Heat the ghee in a tawa or frying pan. Cook each roti over medium heat for about 2 minutes on each side until they start to blister and turn golden brown. Serve hot with the mutton korma.

TWO

From Irn-Bru to Écrevisses

Food has always been important to me—ours was definitely the kind of family that spoke about the options for dinner over breakfast—but there was nothing in my early gastronomic education that could have shaped or predicted the Old Delhi years. My mother was a talented self-taught cook and gifted baker (her pastry and sponges were legendary) but she didn't approve of food that was 'fancy' or 'mucked about with'. This covered all foreign food, dishes containing more than a couple of ingredients, or accompanied by sauce, and anything containing nuts. 'Good plain food' was my mother's highest accolade and reserved for the sacred pairings that appeared at most mealtimes—mince and tatties, eggs and bacon, fish and chips. Until, suddenly liberated by divorce, she enrolled in a Cordon Bleu cookery class and soon, very 'mucked about with' food, invariably with French names, started to appear on our dinner table. This could have been a key moment on what reality TV shows love to call 'my food journey' but by then it was too late for my brother, sister and I; we still regard the Cordon Bleu days as a dark period in our childhood when we would come home from school hoping for the comfort of sausage and mash only to find the fussiness of chicken marengo or duck à l'orange waiting for us. We'd always clean our plates, though—pickiness was never an option in our house—then Mum would ask what we thought. 'It was great, Mum,' we would reply stoically, 'but we wouldn't have it again. Can we have macaroni cheese tomorrow?'

When I was thirteen, I had another opportunity to broaden my culinary horizons when I went on a summer exchange trip to the birthplace of fancy food—France. I stayed in the heart of the Mâcon wine country with a farming family who raised and grew their own food and every mealtime their long wooden kitchen table groaned with enough traditional, rustic fare to shape any budding gastronome. I wish I could say I took one look at the rillettes de porc, roast duck, pickles, creamy gratin dauphinois and salads and instantly knew my destiny. In fact, I squirm to remember the teenage me who took one look and asked for cornflakes—from a family who had never previously bought any food from a shop—then complained that the milk (fresh from the cows in the yard) tasted funny.

Back home, however, undeterred by the prospect of a lifetime of eating dry cereal, and probably just a little influenced by the arrival at my Grammar school of a dreamy long-haired French teacher called Jean Christophe, soon afterwards I decided I would study French at university and devote my life to existentialism. I knew that to be a convincing Francophile, simply wearing a beret and carrying a copy of *L'Étranger* wouldn't suffice; I would also have to embrace the country's food. The following summer I went to stay with a different family and this time I resolved to eat everything madame put in front of me. There were challenges—the snails were a low point, especially as I had to watch them die slowly in their baskets over several days, then endure the smell of them boiling, which had me retching and sweating with appalled anticipation hours before we even sat down to dinner. By then they resembled nothing more offensive than the tiny nugget of rubber at the end of our school pencils drenched in parsley, butter and garlic. When I went to bed that night, I decided if I could stomach 'eraser au beurre persillé', I could probably eat anything. Perhaps that was a turning point; by the end of the three weeks there was much I loved about French food—tomates farcies, tarte tatin, the vast array of breads and patisserie; I even took a few cautious nibbles of saucisson sec and pâté.

That summer was also the first time I ate in a proper restaurant. The nearest I'd ever previously come to eating out was in Cadman's Café in Arbroath, the Scottish east coast port where my parents grew up and the only place we ever went on holiday. We used to stop at Cadman's after swimming to plead for Irn-Bru and 'tablet' (the dangerously addictive Scottish version of fudge). Other specialities were frothy pink milkshake and Scotland's national biscuit, Tunnock's Caramel Log. These we would devour sitting at the Formica tables before begging our grandmother for a bag of bright orange Butter Nut sweets to take home.

At the picturesque stone auberge in the Ardèche where I ate that summer, locals came in search of a celebration of local food rather than a neon-coloured sugar fix and all my previously learned rules of dining went out the window. For a start, we teenagers were treated like adults. Everyone ate at the same long table spread with starchy white linen and groaning with porcelain platters and terrines. We were even permitted to sip at our own glasses of wine. Most of the food on the table was unfamiliar but I was informed I was about to try my first gratin, daube, clafoutis and freshly caught local trout. The highlight was a dish almost the colour of Irn-Bru but which I didn't even recognize after I'd looked it up in my

Larousse Pocket Dictionary. Whatever these 'écrevisses aux tomates' were, I noted, they broke more rules. Diners were allowed, required actually, to eat with their fingers (something that was strictly forbidden at my mother's table), everyone helping themselves from the huge bowl in the centre of the table. I've never eaten crayfish since, but I can still taste it, the delicate white meat, hard won from every tiny claw, and the rich tomato sauce splattered all over the plate, tablecloth and faces of replete and happy diners.

Too soon I was back home, my culinary awakenings cut short—this time I was devastated at the lack of baguette and Brie in our small Cheshire town and pestered my mum for coq au vin. By now, though, the Cordon Bleu experiment was over, so I resolved to find a way back to France; I stocked up on Camus and Sartre, listened to Serge Gainsbourg and dreamed of food with sauce.

When I did eventually return to France, first as a student and later to work, food quickly replaced existentialism as a priority. Before I left Paris for the last time, my landlady gave me a copy of *La Cuisine Pour Tous*, the recipe book traditionally given to new brides. Back home I set about experimenting, cooking for family and friends, the mixed results often received in the 'polite' fashion I recognized from the Cordon Bleu years of my childhood.

Towards the end of my twenties, my feet grew itchier and my palate more curious and after trips to southern Europe, Morocco and India, I'd developed a taste for tapas, tagines, bacalao and masala dosa. Having a family of my own turned out to be a wonderful opportunity to experiment and feed people every day, although my children are not always as polite as I once was when faced with new dishes. I'm lucky my family indulges me in planning holidays primarily as an opportunity to take in new cuisines rather than monuments, museums or landscapes. We've gone on self-catering holidays that involve packing up and shifting almost the entire contents of the kitchen. (I recently came across an old holiday inventory which ran into several pages and listed everything from three types of sugar, bouillon and mincemeat to muffin cases, measuring cups, a food mixer and an electric oven—that was the year we had to take two cars for our annual Himalayan holiday.) The only diary I've ever religiously maintained is my food journal. In it, I plan family meals, document everything we have eaten or might ever conceivably eat, rate new recipes, list meals at restaurants and other people's houses and paste recipes snipped from magazines. It's often the first thing I look at in the morning and the last thing at night.

In theory, by the time we arrived in India in 2005, all set for an adventure, I should have been poised to embark on the culinary quest of a lifetime. Dean had the foreign correspondent's job he'd always wanted, the children were going to learn Hindi and have their horizons well and truly broadened, and I, like the heroine of a book I'd recently read, E. M. Forster's *A Passage to India*, would set out to find 'the real India'. In fact, the visit to Mr Qureshi didn't take place until more than five years later. My first mistake, like Adela's in Forster's novel, was assuming I would blend effortlessly into Indian life.

It started promisingly enough. We arrived in the middle of a suitably sultry and exotic September night and spotted an elephant on the airport road into Delhi. At the Master Paying Guest House, we happily peeled off our Scottish layers and had our first encounter with rackety air-conditioners. Even trying to sleep in temperatures upward of forty degrees centigrade amid frequent power cuts seemed thrillingly exotic. The next morning, we all sipped sweet chai on the balcony and watched the neighbourhood spring to life before embarking upon a love affair with aloo puri for breakfast. As Elizabeth Bishop put it in her poem 'Questions of

Travel', we were glad we hadn't just 'stayed at home and thought of here'.

Our initial enthusiasm was dampened when we discovered that whereas on previous trips to India we had been 'travellers', this time we were 'expats' and in Delhi at least, expats are treated as a suspect subcategory of the country's social stratification system for which special rules apply. Like some potentially dangerous species, we were marshalled into the expensive residential 'colonies' of South Delhi. Our children, we were told, would have to go to an international school where, far from achieving fluency in Hindi, they acquired American accents. As for our social life, Dean was expected to do the rounds of diplomatic cocktail parties and I acquired the most dream-crushing label imaginable—'trailing spouse'. As such I should try to fit a little bit of Mughal-monument spotting into a hectic whirl of yoga, shopping and lunch.

Another aspect of expat life was that for the first time in our lives we were expected to have household staff, and as word got round of new arrivals in the neighbourhood, our doorbell rang constantly with would-be drivers, maids, cooks, gardeners and security guards. Initially, as we all struggled to get used to the heat, constant power cuts and lack of supermarkets, it seemed like a good idea to ease the workload. For me, though, this quickly created problems I hadn't foreseen. The most devastating was that the kitchen was no longer the hub and heart of our family life. Our Edinburgh kitchen had not just been the place where food was prepared, it was where we ate, did homework, ironed school uniforms and shared the day's events. It was where friends gathered to share a bottle of wine and plan camping trips, where book groups met, sometimes even to discuss books, and from where one of our cats escaped and another died. Our new kitchen in Delhi was basically a sliver of space nine feet by six with no windows, ventilation or air conditioning. There was a swing door at either end, one from which our housekeeper appeared with food, the other handily close to the incessant demands of the front door. There was an old steel sink, where all the washing up was done, a cracked marble floor, weevils burrowing relentlessly into every packet of dry food and termites nibbling at cupboards, doors, even my kitchen notebooks. In the absence of any natural light, there was a single bare strip light that bathed both people and food in an unappetizing fluorescent glow. There might as well have been a sign on the door—'Staff only. Keep out!'

I could cope with the occasional yoga class or shopping trip but I wasn't prepared to relinquish my role of creator and provider of good things to eat. In fact, as I became more and more miserable, I started to wonder if my happiness levels were directly related to the amount of time I spent thinking about, preparing and eating food. And so, on a still hot September day, I decided I had to regain some personal equilibrium and seize back some control of the kitchen by making one of our family's favourite dinners—a simple, comforting roast chicken and pasta dish based on a French recipe I'd cut from a magazine years ago. Recreating it in our Delhi kitchen turned out to be anything but simple.

My first stop was the cluster of grim, temporary-looking shops collectively known as E Block Market. As I walked the few hundred yards from our house, I was constantly accosted by people asking if I needed a driver or a maid—why else, their puzzled looks implied, would I be walking and carrying shopping? The 'market' consisted of two or three almost identical, tiny grocery shops, selling piles of Britannia biscuits and the odd imported packet of cornflakes or tin of baked beans. I made my way to the meat shop where, as I waited for my order of chicken, I could hear the sounds of slaughter out back. At the uninspiring Mother Dairy kiosk, I bought milk and tomatoes.

Everything else involved a car journey. First it was off to C Block Market—like an E Block Market with aspirations. Here was Shevik's toyshop, a picture framer's, a children's clothes shop and a grocer who could whistle up pasta and olive oil. To buy the wine I needed I had to scramble down into a dingy basement to jostle with sweaty men in vests and lungis buying their quarter bottles of liquor and suffer suspicious looks at being a lone woman in such an establishment. For basil it was back in the car to get to the Malai Mandir market where the displays of fruit and vegetables were fresh and vibrant but marred by the fact that the market itself was swarming with flies and clustered on the edge of a stinking stream. It had taken me the better part of a day to source the ingredients for a simple family meal and I hadn't even started to cook.

In my desperate attempt to recreate some semblance of 'home', I had forgotten about the first line of the recipe—'Preheat oven to 230°C'. A dish which had always been so comforting to prepare and eat in our cool Edinburgh kitchen turned the poky little Delhi cubbyhole into a furnace and me into a sweating, tearful, defeated heap. By the time we sat down to eat I had no energy for family banter, had completely lost my appetite and was wondering how strong my commitment to ruling the kitchen really was. In my journal, alongside the recipe, I have written 'try again in December' and a forlorn 'gazpacho?'.

My first steps back to cooking hadn't been a success and I knew that claustrophobic kitchen was never going to be anything but a place to spend as little time in as possible. Then, towards the end of our first year, a solution seemed to present itself when we moved to a farmhouse on the outskirts of Delhi. Our new home had peacocks, a swimming pool, and enough room in the garden to play football and tennis. To my delight, there was also a spacious open-plan kitchen/dining room fitted with a full range of modern appliances, and a back door that opened on to a large vegetable patch where I envisaged crops of organic rocket, rhubarb and parsnips.

But after we moved in we discovered that none of the appliances in our kitchen actually worked—they were, our rather regal landlady proudly explained, just for show. 'This area,' she said, waving arms glinting with diamonds and emeralds over a large gleaming workstation in the middle of the room, 'is where madam assembles the food for her guests. The staff, of course, will make the food in the back.' She meant the poky little room at the back of the house with a single gas burner, which we had assumed was an outhouse of the staff quarters. As for madam's vegetable patch, the gardener could never be persuaded to grow anything but mustard leaf, for which, we decided, he must have been the sole supplier for all the surrounding villages.

As we neared the end of the second year of our 'adventure', I was no further forward either in the kitchen or in India. In fact, we were so far off the beaten track, we now had virtually no contact with India or Indian people—apart from the daily, terrifying sight of our landlady striding across the lawn. Even the fruit and vegetable hawkers couldn't face the trek to our home—which friends had aptly nicknamed 'The Bitter End'. But I returned from our summer holiday that year with a stiff upper lip and a renewed resolve to somehow start cooking again. As it turned out, stoicism wouldn't be enough—far from providing a sanctuary, a home that was well on the way to Rajasthan meant a depressing grind of long, bumpy car journeys to the children's school. An electrician had to be summoned most days to keep the house functioning (he, too, was baffled by the showpiece kitchen appliances). The swimming pool never had water in it except when it rained; the house, on the other hand, had been built so far below the water table that it flooded at the mere suggestion of rain and, as a result, in the monsoon we lost most of our furniture. Plus, I discovered, there really is a limit to how much mustard leaf one family can eat.

ROAST CHICKEN WITH PASTA AND TOMATOES

SERVES 4-5

This is a comforting, homey supper dish from a recipe I cut out of a magazine many years ago.

INGREDIENTS

- 500 gms ripe tomatoes, skinned, seeds removed and roughly chopped
- 1 chicken, about 1.5 kg, with skin on, cleaned and dried
- ½ tsp salt
- Freshly ground pepper
- 1 tbsp fresh ginger, grated
- 3 tbsp olive oil
- Juice of one lemon
- 50 ml dry white wine
- 2 garlic cloves, finely chopped
- 400 gms small pasta shapes
- A large handful of basil leaves, chopped

METHOD

Preheat the oven to 230°C. Toss the deseeded and chopped tomatoes in a colander with ½ teaspoon of salt and set aside while you cook the chicken.

Season the inside of the cleaned and dried chicken with salt and pepper and the grated ginger. Place the chicken on a roasting tray and rub the skin with 2 tablespoons of the olive oil and season all over with salt and pepper.

Roast the chicken for 20 minutes, then lower the temperature to 180°C. Pour off any excess fat from the pan and pour a little of the lemon juice and wine over the chicken. Return the chicken to the oven and roast for another 45 minutes, basting every 15 minutes with lemon juice and white wine until the juices from the thigh of the chicken run clear when pierced with a knife.

Around 15 minutes before the chicken is ready, cook the pasta in a large pan of boiling salted water until al dente. Drain the pasta. When the chicken has been roasting for about 1 hour, put the remaining tablespoon of olive oil and the two cloves of chopped garlic into a large frying pan on a low heat. When the garlic starts to sizzle, add the tomatoes and cook on a high heat until the tomato mixture is sauce-like but fairly dry. Add the chopped basil.

Remove the chicken from the oven and on to a chopping board. Add the tomato mixture to the roasting tray then tip in the pasta. Mix well to incorporate everything. When plating, carve the chicken into smallish pieces then place on top of the pasta. Serve with a green salad.

THREE

A Refuge in Old Delhi

In the middle of Hauz Qazi Chowk, a small group of policemen shout and wave their lathis around, trying, and failing, to keep everything moving. Horns blare, bicycle horns tinkle and skinny weather-beaten men in scraps of threadbare cloth wield sticks at equally bony bullocks. Mules stagger with baskets of stones strapped to their backs; shrivelled old women in thin saris balance baskets of herbs and berries on their heads; tethered goats feast on leaves; rickshaw wallahs pedal for their lives to transport overfed traders and their day's purchases. Vendors push rickety carts loaded with mulberries, jal jeera, or ice cream cones packed with ice in wooden barrels; mid-morning snacks are ram laddoos or papri chaat served on a dried-leaf plate. As you emerge dazed from Chawri Bazaar station, you might wonder whether the city's gleaming new metro system, as well as being miraculously efficient in the midst of all the madness, has been fitted with the power to transport passengers back in time.

Many visitors return from Old Delhi depressed by the medieval chaos, filth and hardship of everyday life there. They're appalled at the sight of glue-sniffing children, limbless beggars and the rows of day labourers hunched over their pots and paintbrushes waiting patiently, but usually in vain, for a few hours' work. They recoil from the destitutes with matted hair and clothes stiff with grime who crouch in lines outside restaurants waiting for someone with a soft heart to stop and buy them a meal. Others are horrified by the lack of sanitation and the clouds of flies swarming over uncovered displays of sweets and kebabs. And anyone who comes searching for Shah Jahan's great walled city will leave distraught at the dilapidated state of the area's many historic buildings—though if they pause to look up at the jungle of electrical wiring overhead, they might also marvel that the whole place didn't go up in smoke long ago.

I saw and felt all of this when I first visited Old Delhi. But for me, during our first confusing and difficult months in the south of the city, the area also became a refuge; both from the beautiful but parochial small country we had left and the stifling expat bubble of New Delhi in which we now found ourselves. Dean and I would take off to Old Delhi whenever we needed a break from our dysfunctional farmhouse and lose ourselves in the crowds, a world and several centuries away from our scheming landlady and kitchen full of fake appliances. We would return sweaty and dehydrated but exhilarated, senses overloaded, reminded of why we came to India in the first place. The philosopher Dagobert D. Runes once observed that 'people travel to faraway places to watch, in fascination, the kind of people they ignore at home', but for us, nowhere was this less true than in Old Delhi, where absolutely nothing reminded us of home.

It's true a thick rose-tinted lens is required to visualize Old Delhi's heyday. Little remains of the sprawling havelis with their pleasure gardens, pavilions and fountains; the ladies sipping sherbet in the zenanas are mere ghosts and the moonlight no longer glints off a canal in Chandni Chowk—in fact the canal itself is long gone. The Old Delhi we often lament, though, had a relatively brief golden era. The magnificent walled city built by Emperor Shah Jahan in the mid-seventeenth century was hardly a hundred years old when the Persian invasion of 1739 led by Nadir Shah started the gradual process of destruction and decline of the empire. There was a brief reprieve for the city under early British colonizers who showed no desire to do anything but adopt the lavish lifestyle of the Mughal court, many of whom loved to parade around in Indian clothes and enjoyed a nightly nautch and hookah. A panorama painted by the artist Mazhar Ali Khan in 1846 shows a magnificent city, like a cross between Scheherazade's *One Thousand and One Nights*, and Disney's *Aladdin*, a dreamy island that seems to float above inconsequential lands beyond it. Khan's Chandni Chowk is airy, dotted with elephants and their mahouts, camels and elegant horse-drawn carriages. On either side of the wide boulevard are the qahwa khanas, the teahouses where nobles and intellectuals of the time gathered to pull on their hookah pipes. Now a grim electrical products market, Bhagirath Palace was, to Khan's eye, acres of shady gardens surrounding the white portico-ed mansion of Begum Samru.

Just over a decade later, it was the British who comprehensively wrecked much of what remained of Shahjahanabad in the aftermath of the 1857 First War of Independence. As well as destroying parts of the Red Fort to turn it into barracks, they also demolished all of the buildings within a 400-metre radius of it. At Partition there was another violent exodus and in recent years, many of the remaining Old Delhi families have moved out and their once beautiful homes have been sublet or rented out to small businesses.

And yet, while much of Old Delhi's heritage has been lost,

miraculously, many of its historic buildings have survived, at least partially, the rapacious colonizers and traders, merciless climate and unforgivable neglect. They now mostly provide a poignant, evocative, sometimes completely obscured backdrop to thousands of stores, warehouses and workshops. What was once a begum's palace is now a pickpockets' paradise; vegetable shops nestle in seventeenth-century doorways; sacks of grain spill over haveli courtyards.

My favourite spot to stop for a cup of tea is in one of the hundreds of surprisingly quiet little gullies leading off the wedding market in Kinari Bazaar. A few steps up from the street there's a forgotten courtyard and the remains of a small family temple, probably once part of a modest haveli. The main house is long gone, a tree now grows through the temple and up between the brash modern buildings on either side, but a tea vendor has set up shop in what would have been the tehkhana—the basement area where families used to retreat from the summer heat—and at lunchtime, a biryani vendor neatly lays out his pots and plates on the wall of the disused temple. I occasionally wish the buildings of Old Delhi could be rescued and restored to their former glory and if I had three wishes, the first would be to time travel back to seventeenth-century Delhi. But generally I think it's better for a forgotten courtyard to buzz with today's bustle rather than stand as a perfectly preserved but lifeless relic of the past.

Despite its gradual physical decline as the city's civic authorities fail to provide even the most basic amenities to residents and businesses, Old Delhi has resolutely refused to crumble or give up on its burning desire to make something of itself. Since Mughal times, when the city's caravanserais were full of merchants from Armenia, Persia, Central Asia and Kashmir, fortune hunters have always been drawn to the city. Then, as now, migrant workers flooded in from the surrounding states and beyond, some as part of the vast retinue of the Red Fort, others to work in the households of noblemen in the city. In 1785, it was estimated there were around forty-six main bazaars in the city, including a book and painting market every Friday on the steps of the Jama Masjid and a daily market for slaves, birds and livestock. There was an army of engineers, architects, stonemasons, carpenters and craftsmen of every hue, each with a lane named after them—names that survive today. Maliwara was where the gardeners lived, Kinari Bazaar is still the best place in Delhi to buy haberdashery, the Chamrewali Gali was the home of leather workers. The Katra Ghee Wale, opposite Jama Masjid, marks the spot where the ghee traders once lived. Gali Kababian, home of Karim's restaurant, remains a great place to eat kebabs.

In Old Delhi today, wherever you look there is still someone making, mending or selling. Shoes are repaired with bits of recycled tyre; specks of silver are beaten into wafers of decorative leaf; dupattas are dyed in old oil drums using trays of powdered colours; saris and suits cleaned, stitched, embroidered. Creaking presses still churn out political pamphlets; men bind books by hand, hammer out metal pots. In addition to the well-known paper, jewellery and wedding markets, there are more obscure commodities—an entire warren of lanes near the spice market devoted to Ayurvedic herbs, another whose sole trade is in paan leaves, a lane which sells nothing but goat feed. Vast fortunes are made daily in the gold and spice markets and modest ones aspired to by the constant influx of enterprising migrants.

Some of those fortunes are made from food, in fact in every nook and cranny someone is selling, preparing, cooking or devouring food. Every morning, fruits and vegetables appear and disappear at the Naya Bans market according to harvests and seasons, while over near the Jama Masjid the meat trade is in full swing with vendors hawking buckets of brains and trotters. A little later, the traders of Khari Baoli start on their task of making the world a little spicier. Round the corner there's a narrow lane, Gali Batashan, devoted almost entirely to sweet things where shops sell the sugar, confectionery and preserved fruits that give the gully its name. During festivals, shopkeepers make sugar sculptures of temples, gods and even the Taj Mahal.

Every time I visited, I marvelled at the whole new world of flavours opening up to me. Giant balloons of bhature flying out of vast cauldrons of boiling oil; cooks in Chandni Chowk crouching and peeling potatoes for samosas; men weaving through the crowds with gol gappe, chhole kulche and dahi bhalla arranged into baskets on their heads; men on bicycles with painted tins describing the fresh pakode, chaat, kachoris, kulfi within; the dramatic rituals of the chaat wallahs; the nightly fire and smoke of the kababchis and biryani wallahs, the piles of pillowy naan, the impressive selection of sweets. It was all a liberating leap from the shrink-wrapped, sanitized food culture of home.

But with dire warnings of 'Delhi Belly' and hepatitis ringing in my ears, at first I looked but hardly dared touch the street food. Until one day curiosity and dehydration got the better of me and I stopped at a nimbu-soda wallah opposite the Town Hall on Chandni Chowk. The tiny shop, no more than a metre wide, was almost completely obscured by customers—a sure sign, I decided, of something good, and safe, to consume. Through the crowd I saw a man perched behind a stack of crates full of old-fashioned marble stopper glass bottles. The shop's sign announced that we were in the presence of 'Pt Ved Prakash Lemon Wale' and that the greenish bottles were full of either nimbu soda (₹10) or 'masale wali' (₹12). I ordered a plain soda, initially for the novelty of the bottle, and took a few cautious sips. Soon I was actively relishing the drink itself and wasn't surprised when the owner told me the shop had been there for seven generations.

A little later, I had the good fortune to fall in with a band of street food explorers collectively known as 'Eating Out In Delhi', who encouraged me to try more. With them I ate all over the city; gorged on sticky haleem in Zakir Nagar; kulfi in the teeming markets of Karol Bagh; kachoris somewhere very near the end of the metro's red line; cutlets and kathi rolls in the city's Bengali area, Chittaranjan Park; we even ate our way round India's regional food at the canteens of the Andhra, Maharashtra, Kerala, Assam and Karnataka state bhavans. I felt as if I'd been given the culinary key to the city.

But it was the evening trips to Old Delhi with the group, some of the most gluttonous hours of my life, that I loved most. Our first stop was always Bade Mian's hundred-year-old kheer shop—we ate dessert first just in case they were sold out of their famous rice pudding by the time we'd finished. A few yards further along, on the corner of Gali Qasim Jan, we joined the crowds waiting for Moinuddin's meltingly soft beef kebabs. Back in Chawri Bazaar, where by now the traders had shut for the night and only the brightly lit food stalls still shone, we stopped at Hira Lal's chaat stand for 'kulle chaat'—tomatoes, cucumbers, bananas, potatoes, hollowed out and stuffed with pomegranate seeds, chickpeas, lemon and spices. Despite groaning stomachs, these were usually mere hors d'oeuvres. Still to come, in the nightly food extravaganza of Matia Mahal, would be chicken korma, biryani, and the lethally sweet and rich bread pudding, shahi tukda.

However, it was during a trip out of Delhi with the group that I suddenly felt the culinary ground shift beneath my feet. Hemanshu, Eating Out In Delhi's organizer, suggested we broaden our horizons with a thirty-six-hour binge in Amritsar. As well as being the most important Sikh pilgrimage site in the country, he explained, the town was also the street food capital of India. So when we arrived one freezing February morning on the overnight train from Delhi, instead of heading straight for the glorious Golden Temple to feed our souls, our first stop was a ramshackle roadside dhaba by the name of 'All India Fames', where a swarm of flies had just clocked on for the day shift. We parked ourselves at a tatty plastic table inches from the fumes and filth of the road. Behind a grubby counter, several turbaned men were chopping vegetables, hurling dough and slathering handfuls of Amul butter on to frisbeesized disks of bread, which were flying out of a tandoor that looked as if it may have been around since Guru Nanak was a lad. In front of me were a metal plate and spoon, perhaps not the cleanest—I could see a skinny boy rinsing dishes in the gutter—and the meal it held was an unpromising-looking brown sludge accompanied by a kulcha dripping with butter.

I was wary but also cold and famished. We hadn't eaten anything for over eighteen hours apart from some chai on the train. Cautiously, and with no hope or expectation beyond silencing my growling stomach, I broke off a small piece of the bread and scooped up some of the chickpeas. It took a couple of mouthfuls before I noticed the extraordinary texture of the kulcha—buttery, flaky shards, as if the finest Parisian feuilleté had been combined with a perfectly spiced nugget of soft potato. Then the chhole— melting, nutty, vibrant pulses—spicy yet soothing. A third element on the plate brought it all together—a sour tamarind sauce cutting brilliantly through the buttery bread and creamy chickpeas, making the whole dish sing its heart out.

I was speechless, at least until I'd devoured five more kulche, savouring every startling mouthful, but it wasn't long before I realized that the breakfast I'd just wolfed down, courtesy of a small dhaba in a forlorn backstreet of Amritsar, was one of the best things I'd eaten in years. I felt, as M. F. K. Fisher once did, 'a kind of harmony, with every sensation and emotion melted into one chord of well-being'.

I looked hard at the 'kitchen'. How did such a divine dish come from such unpromising surroundings? How did that threadbare old man tossing dough manage to produce perfect flaky pastry in temperatures which fluctuate from zero to fifty degrees, when everyone from Auguste Fauchon to Nigella Lawson knows that you can only make good pastry if your kitchen, ingredients and hands are constantly as cool as a slab of marble?

When I asked the staff if there was someone I could talk to about the place and the food, I was pointed in the direction of an austere-looking Sikh man sitting on an upturned bucket, peeling his way through a mountain of potatoes. Kanwaljit Singh, I was told, was the third-generation owner of the dhaba. I tried, in my beginner's Hindi, to convey how much I had enjoyed the food, aware that 'bahut lazeez hai' didn't really do it justice, then bombarded him with questions. He looked at me suspiciously but seemed to decide, on balance, that I probably wasn't from the tax department and agreed to show me around.

As we walked over to the bread counter, Kanwaljit told me about his grandfather, Jaswant Singh, who had started the business over sixty years ago, selling his chhole kulche from a cart which he pushed around Amritsar's old city. Over time, his reputation spread and eventually, in 1992, the family established a permanent dhaba here on Maqbool Road.

Jaginder Singh, or 'Baba', who claims to make up to 1,000 kulche a day, 3,000 on Sundays, never deviating from Grandfather Singh's recipe, has been getting up at 5.30 every morning for the past thirty-five years to fire up the tandoor. The secret of the sensational bread is very simple, he told me, 'Our kulcha is more flaky than anywhere else because we fold our dough six to seven times and spread ghee between every layer.'

It took a little persuasion to get Baba and Kanwaljit to show me how they make the kulche but eventually they agreed to let me watch. First, Baba made a simple soft dough from white flour, salt and water, which he then rolled out into a rectangle. Liberal amounts of ghee were scooped from a can and slathered over the top of the dough with a sprinkling of flour, and rubbed to crumbliness. The next stage was straight out of École Lenôtre—Baba carefully folded up the bottom third of the pastry, then folded the top third down over that (often described by pastry chefs as a 'business letter fold'). He repeated the process seven times, his movements sure and confident, and then held up the finished slab for me to inspect the hundreds of layers he had created. He left the dough to rest for a while then broke off small balls of the dough, pushed lumps of spiced potato into the centre, and rolled it into a flat disc. Each dinner plate-sized kulcha was then carefully placed on the sides of the searing tandoor and baked until golden brown and crisp.

I think we may have spent twenty-four of our thirty-six hours in Amritsar eating and perhaps thirty minutes at the Golden Temple, but I certainly didn't feel cheated. We ate many wonderful dishes on the streets of Amritsar and met many remarkable men who make them. Like Balbir Singh, who has been cooking tandoori fish for over forty years and was once approached by the Oberoi Hotel in Delhi to work in their kitchen. Or the Kesar Da Dhaba who turn dal-making into an art form, or the lassis we drank that were thick enough to stand our spoons in. But it is the kulche that will stay with me forever and the memory of Baba, who has never left Amritsar and yet, in the heat, dust, flies and filth of the street, turns out pastry worthy of a Parisian bakery.

BABA SINGH'S AMRITSARI KULCHA

MAKES 8

I couldn't resist trying to make Baba Singh's flaky flatbread. I knew it would never be as good as his—after all, he has been perfecting his technique for over thirty years. Nevertheless and despite the fact that I don't have a searing hot tandoor in my kitchen, these kulche were delicious. I have adapted his recipe slightly, incorporating techniques I would use to make puff pastry to retain the flakiness of the bread. At All India Fames in Amritsar, the kulche are served with chickpeas and a tamarind sauce (see Chapter 5 for similar recipes) but they are wonderful to eat all by themselves with lashings of salty butter.

INGREDIENTS

Kulcha dough

500 gms plain flour

1 tsp salt

250-300 ml water

100 gms ghee mixed with a tablespoon of plain flour to make a thick paste

Kulcha stuffing

250 gms potatoes, boiled and mashed

150 gms cauliflower, chopped into tiny pieces

1 small onion, finely chopped

2 small green chillies, finely chopped

2 tsp fresh ginger, grated

½ tsp red chilli powder, or to taste

1 tsp garam masala

1 tsp salt

A handful of fresh coriander, finely chopped

....

METHOD

In a large bowl, mix together the flour, salt and enough water to form a soft, smooth dough. Knead for about 5 minutes, wrap in cling film and rest in the fridge for 30 minutes. When the dough has rested, roll it out into a large rectangle with the shorter edges at the top and bottom. Spread one quarter of the ghee/flour mixture over the surface of the rectangle. Fold the top third of the rectangle over the middle third then fold the lower third back up over that (like folding a business letter). Turn the folded dough so that the shorter edges are again at the top and bottom and repeat the rolling, spreading ghee and folding. Repeat the rolling and folding four times in all, then wrap in cling film and rest in the fridge for 30 minutes.

While the dough is resting, make the kulcha stuffing by mixing together all the ingredients in a bowl.

When the dough has rested and the stuffing is ready, heat the oven to 230°C and place a large baking sheet on the middle shelf. Lightly flour your work surface and cut the dough into eight equal pieces. When I watched Baba make his kulche, at this point he rolled each piece into a ball then pushed the stuffing into the centre. I did this with the first batch but found the end result was less flaky. For the second trial I rolled each of the eight pieces without any more kneading, flat, into a rectangular/oblong shape and then placed a tablespoon of the stuffing mixture in the centre. For this method, fold the top third of the rectangle down over the stuffing then the bottom third up over that. Roll this rectangle out to about ½ centimetre thick. Place as many kulche as you can fit without crowding on the hot baking sheet (I did two at a time) and bake until the bread is well-browned and puffed up in places. The timing will depend on your oven. I used an electric oven and it took about 8 minutes. Repeat with each piece of dough. Serve, very hot, dripping with salty Amul butter.

FOUR

Independence Day in Sadar Bazaar

After teasing us for several weeks, the rains finally arrived in glorious torrential showers, and the parched world of Delhi opened its mouth wide to drink it all in. Sunsets were accompanied by vast bruised skies; roads flowed like rivers and everywhere a hundred shades of glossy green popped out from the dusty grey. From about mid-April, everyone had been glued to the Mausam Bhawan forecasts, seizing on any sign that the monsoon would be a good one. When the rains finally crashed on to the coast of Kerala, a billion people heaved a sigh of relief, and followed it with a subcontinental wave of expectation as they watched the bulging black clouds make their way across the country. All was well with our world—we knew the rivers would fill up, trees would sprout new growth, crops would be planted and harvested and there would be food to buy—for one more year at least.

The monsoon season is India at its most dramatic, when rivers can burst banks and sweep away whole villages. It is also a time of romance, and the waiting for rain prompts poetry, monsoon weddings and Bollywood actresses frolicking in wet saris. In

Dariba Kalan, Old Delhi's silver market, a two-hundred-year-old perfume shop, Gulab Singh Johrimal, has even managed to bottle the essence of a nation's longing for rain. One of the shop's owners once dreamily described their gill attar to me as 'the smell of the earth after the first shower of monsoon rain, the fragrance of earth breathing and coming back to life'.

Independence Day is the one day of the year when monsoon rain is not welcome and on the morning of 15 August, my phone bleeped with a message—'pls pray for rain to stop'. I looked out at the deeply troubled sky and fat raindrops falling on the Ashoka tree outside our bedroom window. A paper kite had become entangled in the electrical wires, slapping wetly on the glass with every gust of wind, reminding me that the day's plan to fly kites in Old Delhi could be in danger.

I had just returned from our summer holiday in Scotland believing I had managed to discover the truth about Ashok and Ashok, perhaps even stumbled on the origin of their famous recipes. Goggia Uncle's korma certainly bore an uncanny resemblance to the Ashok version and I was enjoying the stories about the founders—it was fun to think of the Ashoks rehabilitated by mutton korma. I pictured a high stakes evening around a poker table when one of the Ashoks found himself on a winning streak and the moment in the early hours when he became the unexpected owner of a local restaurant. As someone more used to dishing out punishment than hot dinners, he naturally turned for help to the man whose korma was the talk of the basti. Who knows, perhaps he even applied a little pressure to extract the recipe? I imagined Ashok looking over Goggia Uncle's shoulder as he cooked his mutton korma, as I had recently done, trying not to miss anything and willing the 'haath ki baat' to be transmitted to his own hands. I could also visualize Goggia Uncle's unblinking contemptuous eyes on Ashok as he took his first faltering steps at the stove. Once he'd mastered the mutton korma, word must have spread fast of the two Ashoks' food, making them better known for their delicious korma than anything else. Then, when they died, I imagined it was left to the next generation not only to maintain the shop's culinary reputation but to quietly cultivate its shady mystique, explaining the combination of world-class food and scowling staff that most people experience on a visit to Ashok and Ashok.

I was so pleased with myself for having stumbled on this most colourful piece of Old Delhi culinary lore, I almost missed the little comment on my blog which would burst my bubble. The commenter's name was Amit Arora and he simply said that he was the son of one of the original Ashoks. I phoned him as soon as I got back to Delhi and was informed, before I'd even had a chance to tell him what I'd discovered, that everything I'd heard about his father was 'TOTALLY CRAP!' When I did manage to get a word in, he told me the story of the card game was 'TOTALLY WRONG' as was any suggestion that his father might have been a gangster. Quite soon I had the clear impression that Amit Arora was a man who spoke mainly in capital letters. 'NO!' he said. 'MY FATHER WAS NOT A GANGSTER!'

Ashok Arora, he told me, was the man on the right of the portrait I'd seen hanging in the shop in Basti Harphool Singh (the one on the left was Ashok Bhatia). Arora had been born in Haridwar in the mid-1960s, the son of a refugee from Peshawar, but moved to Delhi as a young man to try and make something of himself. There he married Amit's mother, Kamlesh, and, in those pre-DVD days, made a living from screening videos in his one-room home in Sadar Bazaar and charging people to watch. He opened Ashok and Ashok in January 1984 in partnership with his friend Ashok Bhatia but the partnership came to an abrupt end in 1997 with Ashok Arora's sudden death. Amit then ended our conversation, promising to show me how the korma is really made and issuing an invitation that sounded more like a command—'COME ON 15 AUGUST, WE'LL FLY KITES FROM THE ROOF—YOU WILL LOVE IT.'

But that year's Independence Day patang bazi was threatening to be a washout. The day had started out wet when Prime Minister Manmohan Singh arrived in Old Delhi for his annual televised address to the nation under a canopy of black cloud. And as he spoke from behind a bulletproof shield on the ramparts of the Red Fort, he looked out over a sea of rain hoods and umbrellas stretching down Chandni Chowk beyond the Sri Digambar Jain Lal Mandir. By late morning there was a sudden break in the showers and we made a dash for it—Dean had decided to take no chances with the gangster myth and was accompanying me to my meeting with the Aroras—but when we stepped outside, the air was like hot breath. The Metro was full of young families in their holiday best—husbands with slicked-back hair and new wristbands from the Raksha Bandhan festival a few days earlier; wives in glittery saris trying to control both their unruly pallus and children. When we emerged from Chawri Bazaar station, we found the streets heavily waterlogged (it doesn't take much to overwhelm Old Delhi's fragile and antiquated drainage system), and the clouds low, almost pitch black. But residents still seemed to be in a festive mood. I watched a young dad in a rickshaw juggle a pile of kites and two small wriggling sons, who looked like they would burst with excitement.

In Old Delhi, the kite battles are fiercely fought; from early morning most families are on their roofs, engaged in combat with their neighbours. The kites are made from brightly coloured paper attached to a thin bamboo frame and the aim is to cut down as many of your opponents' kites as possible, with some using a special, lethal glass-coated string called maanjha. In Lal Kuan, the kite shops were still doing big business catering to the meteorological optimists, despite the soggy fragments plastered to the streets providing ample evidence that their hopes were likely to be dashed.

As we made our way to Sadar Bazaar, on either side of the street were vendors of monsoon comfort food—deep-fried pakoras, samosas and jalebis—doing a roaring trade. Carts were piled high with sticky clumps of dates, the traditional food with which Muslims break their fast—and a reminder that Ramzan was still in full swing.

We had arranged to meet Amit outside Ashok and Ashok but by the time we turned into Subhas Chowk, the rain was bucketing down again and we were soaked. We huddled under the shop's awning to wait, watching the water cascading along the gutters. Soon, a tall, beefy young man wielding an umbrella was coming towards us, then leading us into a small lane further up the hill where we had to navigate huge puddles before following him into a narrow dingy staircase. Once inside we were plunged into total darkness and we had to feel our way along the grimy stone walls. On the second floor, Amit took us through a door into a small room where his mother, Kamlesh, was waiting. Once in the room, I had a chance to take a proper look at Amit. There was no doubt about whose son he was—standing in front of me was a twenty-eight-year-old jeans and T-shirt version of the man in the portrait behind the counter at Ashok and Ashok. He was tall, over six feet, well built, with a jutting jaw like his father's. His English was perfect, a product, he told us later, of a private school education, and he had a tangible nervous energy, never sitting or standing still for a moment. He towered over his tiny mother, who was petite and meek, with a ready smile that revealed not a single tooth.

I was keen to get on to the topic of mutton korma but Amit clearly had something else on his mind. He ushered us into his mother's bedroom, a space not much bigger than the large bed that dominated it. The rain was still pouring outside and the room was steamy. Amit apologized that the air conditioner wasn't working. 'The rats ate through the cables,' he shrugged. He told us to make ourselves comfortable on the bed and issued us with soft drinks and crisps. He started to fiddle with a laptop, stopping every now and then to make sure we were doing as we'd been told—'SIT! EAT! COME ON, YAAR, EAT!'—before ordering us to look at the screen. We watched for a few moments a grainy clip of what appeared to be a crowd milling around at a party. It was, Amit explained, a home movie of his twelfth birthday that had been held in a tent in the lane below where we were sitting and to which, judging by the number of guests, the entire population of Sadar Bazaar had been invited. The shaky camcorder followed Amit around the room and frequently zoomed in on his face as he squirmed in his garland of banknotes. We all laughed as we watched relatives pinch his cheeks, push cake into his mouth and press money envelopes on to him. Suddenly, an imposing man came into the shot, moving slowly through the crowd.

'LOOK! LOOK! TELL ME!' Amit commanded. 'DOES MY FATHER LOOK LIKE A GANGSTER?'

My experience of gangsters, admittedly, is limited to a box set of *The Sopranos* but what I saw was a man who wouldn't be out of place playing the baddie on a TV drama. He was solidly built and at least a head and broad pair of shoulders above the rest of the guests.

'NO WAY WAS HE A GANGSTER! LOOK! LOOK!'

I made a few non-committal noises and asked him where he thought the gangster rumours had come from. 'He was so strong,' said Amit. 'He can't tolerate bad things. He was straightforward. If somebody misbehaves with a girl and he sees, he used to beat them. My dad was like, he has his own terms, he was very disciplined. He was a man of his word, he has his own way, if he doesn't like someone he never serves the food.' But not a gangster? 'He was not a gangster, but people used to fear him.'

What kind of father was he? I wondered. It was important to him that his only son should get a good education, Amit said. He sent Amit to an English school in South Delhi and expected him to do well. 'He beat me when I came second,' Amit said, with pride. He never wanted his son to take over the shop, though; he wanted him to go into business.

Amit and his mother reminisced about Ashok and Ashok's heyday in the 1980s when politicians, actors and cricketers flocked to the joint for their korma fix. Amit said his father even had offers to go and set up a branch in Singapore but turned them down. After we had watched the video, Amit laid out lunch on the bed—chicken korma, biryani and naan, all of which had been brought in. It wasn't as good as Ashok and Ashok's food but I took it as a cue to broach the subject of the mutton korma recipe again. Amit insisted that the three dishes made at the restaurant were his father's recipes. He remembered watching his father experiment at home; his food had a special magic that even his mother's didn't have. 'He has got the touch. Imagine my mom makes a food, I never liked it, but on the same food my dad used to do something, and it was like wow!' Even the food served today at Ashok and Ashok, which I had loved so much, is, he said, a pale imitation of his father's. 'Trust me, the taste of Ashok and Ashok at my dad's time was even two times better than now.' His father passed the recipes on to him, he said, and he hoped one day to open his own restaurant, maybe in South Delhi. He couldn't show me how to make mutton korma today, he said, but he definitely knew the recipe and would show me next time. He still seemed more concerned with trying to clear his father's name, constantly repeating, 'HE WASN'T A GANGSTER!'

After we'd eaten, Amit gave us the family photo albums to flick through—hundreds of family snapshots of Ashok, Kamlesh and their son. Many of the pictures had been taken in the room where we were sitting but in almost every snap, the room looked different. Amit explained that his father used to redecorate their home every Diwali. From the faded photos I could see that while the swirling garish headboard of the bed we were sitting on remained the same, the walls and cupboards underwent a regular dramatic makeover. In some snaps there were gold and silver zigzags, in others, every square inch was covered with mirrors. His father died, Amit said, just a few months after that birthday party in 1997. With no male members of the family to take over the Arora share of the lucrative korma shop, apart from Amit, who wasn't old enough at the time, the Bhatias took control of the business, agreeing to pay a monthly retainer to Arora's widow. I looked around. On the Diwali before he died, he had apparently chosen a dull mottled grey veneer to cover all the cupboards.

As I inwardly agonized over a tactful way to ask the obvious question, Dean suddenly blurted out, 'Do you mind me asking how your father died?' Expecting Amit's answer to be a story of sudden illness or heart attack, we were both shocked when Amit calmly and mysteriously said, 'That's a story I can't tell!' Perhaps realizing he had said too much, he then turned to the window as if looking for a way out. He found it. 'Come on, yaar, it's stopped raining, let's go outside!'

Every roof was full of people—all gazing up as if there had been news of approaching UFOs—united in the simple pleasure of keeping a kite off the ground, and from Sadar Bazaar to the distant Jama Masjid, the sky was full of what looked like an enormous, unruly flock of colourful migrating birds. Keen to join in, I decided my questions could wait for another day. Today there was something more important than korma, gangsters and recipes—there were kites to fly. Perhaps feeling he still hadn't done enough to clear his father's name, Amit made us promise to come back for the Janmashtami celebrations. 'YOU'RE GONNA LOVE IT.'

A week later, in our South Delhi neighbourhood, the Janmashtami celebrations for the birth of Lord Krishna began with an early morning parade of elephants, camels, horses and the requisite ragtag marching bands belting out the tuneless cacophony that Dean describes as 'like music, but different'. By the time we reached the Metro in the early evening, it seemed as if the whole city was out on the streets but the groups of high-spirited young men weren't there to honour Krishna. They were on their way, as were thousands of others across the capital, to Old Delhi to show their support for an old man in a Nehru cap who was publicly starving himself to death at the Ramlila Ground on the edge of Old Delhi.

That monsoon, a seventy-four-year-old activist named Anna Hazare had adopted the language of Mahatma Gandhi in a one-man bid to rid India of corruption. Hazare's movement had been gaining momentum throughout the country since the beginning of the year and a few days before Janmashtami he had announced that his was a 'fast unto death', nothing less than 'a second freedom struggle'. The scale of the anti-corruption protests that had followed rattled the government and the prime minister, Manmohan Singh, had even addressed the issue directly in his Independence Day speech. 'Corruption manifests itself in many forms,' he was forced to admit to the country. 'Funds meant for schemes for the welfare of the common man end up in the pocket of government officials. In some other instances, government discretion is used to favour a selected few. There are also cases where government contracts are wrongfully awarded to the wrong people. We cannot let such activities continue unchecked.' The following day, as Hazare was about to begin his hunger strike, he was arrested and thrown into Delhi's notorious Tihar Jail. This served merely to fan the revolutionary flames, especially when the canny campaigner refused to leave the jail until he was allowed to carry out his fast in public. The country erupted, millions poured out on to the streets and the authorities were forced to capitulate and allow Hazare to stage his fast in full public glare on a stage in the Ramlila Ground.

On the Metro that Janmashtami evening, the atmosphere was electric. At one stop a group of young men wearing bandanas burst into the carriage shouting 'Inquilab Zindabad', a slogan associated with the struggle against British rule. 'For sixty-four years they've taken the rotis out of our mouths,' shouted a man whose face was covered in the orange, white and green stripes of the Indian flag. The anger was aimed at everyone in the ruling classes, up to and including the once universally revered political family of the Gandhis, now being accorded rodent status. 'Huha, Huha! Rahul Gandhi chuha!' chanted one group. 'Inquilab Zindabad!' roared back the other passengers.

When we left the Metro we asked Rahul, our rickshaw driver, to take a detour via the Ramlila Ground before heading to the Aroras'. As soon as we passed through Turkman Gate, we were swept up in crowds of young men all wearing little white topis with the words 'I Am Anna' stamped on the side, each with a tale of corruption to share—the dhaba wallahs who pay up to a quarter of their earnings to the police to be allowed to stay open as well as feeding the local constables for free; the 'donations' paid to secure a place for a child at school; the rickshaw wallahs, like Rahul, who pay 20 per cent of a paltry salary to the police or risk having their tyres slashed. The police themselves pay bribes to join the force in the first place and then spend most of their working lives paying it back. As one young man had told *The Times of India:* 'We have to pay the police constable a bribe to work, the MCD [Municipal Council of Delhi] clerk a bribe to get a birth certificate and the government hospital ward boy to ensure that an attendant looks after my pregnant wife.'

Korma, Kheer and Kismet

The atmosphere on Asaf Ali Road was almost carnival-like with a high-spirited sea of people winding its way towards the Ramlila Ground. There were trucks loaded with people singing and chanting; young men on motorbikes trailing flags and shouting 'Inquilab Zindabad'; every few steps there was a stall selling Anna hats and flags and, as we drew close to the entrance to the Ramlila Ground, opportunistic, if incongruous, snack sellers lined the route.

Inside the Ramlila Ground it was swampy underfoot after the day's rains, full of mostly ordinary young men, many of them perhaps losing a day's wages to support the movement. But the middle classes were also out in force, we even bumped into two of our elderly neighbours wearing Anna hats and T-shirts and quietly expressing a hope for an end to the insidious daily corruption blighting every one of India's billion inhabitants.

Many were fasting in solidarity with their leader and one man had pledged to remain blindfolded until the Lokpal Bill was passed, declaring, 'I covered my eyes the moment I entered the venue yesterday morning and haven't eaten since. A new India is awakening thanks to Anna and I want to open my eyes only to this new country.' Another had had a burning lamp attached to his head for the past week, even managing to sleep without extinguishing the flame, and planned to keep it lit until Hazare's demands were met.

Anna Hazare was being hailed as a new Gandhi, even a reincarnation of Krishna and saviour of the nation. The mood was not just hopeful but prematurely celebratory. Hazare broke his fast a few days later with a glass of sweetened coconut water, after forcing the Indian government into seemingly unprecedented concessions. An anti-corruption ombudsman was to be appointed in every state; the new anti-corruption legislation would be applicable to all levels of bureaucracy; and a citizens' charter to address complaints would be introduced. The people had spoken, and the government, for once, it seemed, had listened. The following day, though, the majority of Indians went straight back to what one man described to *The Guardian* as, 'All your life you pay for things that should be free.'

Leaving behind Anna Hazare playing Krishna as warrior king, we headed back through Turkman Gate where, as we made our way to Sadar Bazaar, we found the usually dark, shuttered streets in a party mood, celebrating the god's more youthful side. Bells were ringing in the area's Krishna temples where idols of the lord had been bathed in milk and honey and dressed in their finery to celebrate his birthday. Many streets were hosting parties and every little gully seemed to beam with fairy lights and flowers. We stopped to watch a man dressed as Radha, singing and dancing on a makeshift stage in front of a small crowd. One ditty, according to Rahul, expressed the following sentiment—'Don't give me milk, don't give me apples, give me hash.'

When we arrived in Basti Harphool Singh, the small grid of streets had already been swept clean and one entire street had been tented and floodlit, making the buildings on either side look like a theatre set. As we neared the Aroras' home, Amit was peering out from his balcony and ran down to greet us and guide us round the festivities. Inside the tent, hundreds were shuffling past living tableaux depicting Krishna at each stage of his life, as cowherd, flute-player, romantic, wooer of milkmaids, lover of all things dairy. As we stopped to watch a group of young girls dressed as gopis fluttering around an awkward-looking boy in Krishna garb, Amit told us that although the Basti Harphool Singh Janmashtami was a popular and long-standing Hindu event, the neighbourhood had very few Hindu families left and most of the visitors came in from other areas. We continued on to another area of the tent where a procession of VIPs and dignitaries were being 'felicitated'. To our great surprise and embarrassment, Dean and I were also invited on to the VIP stage to receive garlands of marigolds and a framed picture of Radha and Krishna, for no other reason, apparently, than being the first foreigners to visit the neighbourhood Janmashtami celebrations in its thirty-five-year history.

Once we had congratulated the organizers on an excellent event, taken several turns round the tent and grinned widely at being felicitated, we went back to the Aroras' house for another picnic on Kamlesh's bed. Over pizza and cream cakes, I tried to turn the conversation round to mutton korma but mother and son continued to lament the changing demographic of their neighbourhood. They were desperate, they said, to move out of the area. They had no friends or family left nearby. Amit said, 'My mother takes the train once a year on Raksha Bandhan to visit her family in Faridabad, otherwise she stays at home. Her only friend now is the TV.' Kamlesh's greatest fear was that the neighbourhood was hampering her son's marriage prospects. Amit, although seemingly in no rush to get hitched, was also worried that if he stayed in Basti Harphool Singh, he had no chance of ever finding a wife. 'What girl wants to come and live here?' he asked. 'Auto drivers won't come here,' he said, 'what hope of bringing a wife?'

As we left the Aroras' that night, I felt melancholy; pessimistic about ordinary people ever living without corruption and certain that the days of kite-flying, Krishna and mutton korma in Sadar Bazaar were numbered. But as we turned the corner, Amit tried to lift our spirits. 'Can you imagine what it's like at Diwali?' he shouted down from the balcony. 'YOU'RE GONNA LOVE IT!'

As it turned out I never got to spend Diwali with the Aroras in Basti Harphool Singh and by the following Janmashtami, they would be gone, having swapped their rat-infested Old Delhi tenement for a brand-new apartment across the river. I never did discover whether the Aroras had the original recipe for Ashok and Ashok's mutton korma and as the months, then years, passed, I simply forgot to ask. I eventually no longer even cared if Ashok Arora or his partner had an unsavoury past. Amit and Kamlesh became friends I visited for festivals or whenever I went to eat at Ashok and Ashok. Kamlesh always plied me with food and sent my children off with five-hundred-rupee notes. I took my sons to the family's small pool room where they played with Amit under a portrait of Ashok resembling Elvis Presley. I continued to visit the Aroras after they shifted out of Sadar Bazaar. Each time, Amit would tell me about his new business schemes—selling T-shirts or sportswear. Always, though, he would remind me of his main ambition, to follow in his father's footsteps. 'I'm still looking for somewhere to open Ashok and Ashok Mark 2.'

ALOO TIKKI

A perfect snack for monsoon time—or anytime!

MAKES 4

INGREDIENTS

    500 gms potatoes, boiled in their skins
    ½ tsp roasted ground cumin
    ½ tsp dried mango powder
    ¼ tsp red chilli powder
    ½ tsp salt
    1 tbsp plain flour
    4 tbsp breadcrumbs (optional, but the Japanese 'Panko' variety make the tikkis nice and crisp)
    2-3 tbsp sunflower oil

50 gms fresh peas, boiled until tender

Yogurt, coriander chutney and tamarind chutney to serve

METHOD

Grate the potatoes into a large bowl and add the cumin, mango powder, chilli powder, salt and plain flour. Mix well then adjust the seasoning to taste. Divide into 4 and shape each portion into a ball. Make a depression in the ball with your thumb and fill with ¼ of the peas. Fold the potato around the peas, roll into a ball then flatten slightly to form a tikki. Pat some breadcrumbs (if using) all over the surface of the tikkis.

Heat a tablespoon of oil in a frying pan over a high heat and when hot add the tikkis. Cook for one minute then flip over and cook for another minute. Reduce the temperature and cook the tikkis until very crisp, flipping them over every minute or so.

When the tikkis reach your desired level of crispness, serve with your favourite chutney.

FIVE

Homesick Restaurants

I have never eaten a bad aloo tikki but I have eaten some glorious ones. Over in Katra Neel cloth market, just off the Fatehpuri end of Chandni Chowk, Gopal Kishen Gupta has raised the simple act of frying potatoes to an art form. It's easy to miss his miniscule stall as it is partly hidden by what looks like a Mughal gate at the street's entrance in which it is embedded. But plenty do manage to find their way to Gupta's, particularly during the monsoon season when people crave salty, spicy, fried food. Hungry crowds usually start to build up way before Gupta is ready to serve them but he refuses to be hurried by even the most pleading of eyes. First, he arranges all his metal tins containing mashed potato, chutneys, sauces and spices in front of him. Then he cleans his giant tawa and melts some ghee. While the ghee heats up, he forms patties of potato and lays them around the edge of the tawa. As customers shout orders, he moves the patties into the pool of sizzling ghee at the centre and leaves them to cook. He prides himself on a very crisp aloo tikki so he lets his patties fry for longer than most other vendors. When he finally does start to release the tikkis, for the urgently carb-starved, Gupta will quickly slap the patty between two slices of white bread and hand it over; if you can bear to wait, he'll turn the tikkis into a plate of chaat. First, on a dried-leaf plate he crushes the patty lightly into jagged bite-sized pieces. To this he adds, according to the customer's preference, any or all of the following—sweet tamarind sauce, spicy green chilli chutney, red chilli chutney, yogurt, fresh coriander. Each mouthful first shatters saltily in the mouth like Heston Blumenthal's triple-cooked fries, followed by the softly spiced fluffy interior, sweetness from the tamarind sauce, sourness from the yogurt, and a lasting kick from the chilli. A party in a plate.

What makes Old Delhi's street food so good? Why can I no longer imagine life without Gupta's aloo tikki, Moinuddin's beef kebabs, Ashok and Ashok's korma? It's partly, I believe, because many of the vendors' dishes are like supercharged home cooking, full of everything nutritionists nag us about—sugar, fat, salt and carbohydrates—designed to provide solace as well as sustenance to diners with limited means. Many of these are migrant workers, mostly from poor rural areas who flock to the city to work as rickshaw wallahs, porters and day labourers, send most of their earnings back home, sleep where they drop, and can often only afford to eat one cheap meal a day. For a few rupees, that meal has to provide enough nutrition and energy to keep them on their feet all day, but it also has to soothe the soul and revive flagging spirits. Men who only have a few rupees to spend on dinner spend them wisely. They're likely to be discerning, choosing the vendor who throws in an extra piece of bread, or sprinkling of spice, whose bedmi aloo reminds them of their mothers', whose pickled yam tingles on the tongue long after they've wiped clean the plate.

Many street food vendors started off as migrants themselves so are well equipped to serve hungry and homesick diners. Sitaram Diwan Chand's shop in Paharganj is the home of one of Delhi's favourite comfort foods—chhole bhature. I once spent a very happy morning there eating and chatting to Pran Kohli, the shop's current owner, about their history and watching them make their famous dish. He told me the business was started by his grandfather, Diwan Chand, who arrived in Delhi from what is now Pakistan, at the time of Partition in 1947 with little more than his recipe for chhole bhature to his name. For thirty years Diwan Chand and his son Sitaram sold their popular dish from a handcart before moving into their present site—a small shop near the Imperial Cinema.

With my love of anything deep-fried, I found Sitaram Diwan Chand's balloon-sized bhatura easy to love and even a lifetime of indifference to pulses was quickly overturned by their creamy, softly spiced chickpeas. Every mouthful was memorable but the ones where I managed to cram in paneer-laced bhatura, chickpeas, potatoes, onion *and* pickled carrot all at the same time made me wonder if I'd discovered a flavour more delicious than umami.

In those early days, I was constantly amazed at the range of flavours and textures I experienced at the city's street stalls. It was thrilling to watch the men (and in Old Delhi it's always men who make the food) at work, the precision and sureness that comes from generations of practice. I also loved the non-stop drama that accompanied every meal—eating milk cake sitting on an old car seat in Kucha Ghasi Ram, wondering if the barber opposite always manages to avoid slicing his customers' necks with his cut-throat razor; eating omelette with chai at a tiny shop near the Jama Masjid in the early hours of Eid ul-Adha, surrounded by men in starched white kurtas waiting for the call to prayer; arriving at number 1210 Chandni Chowk at the exact moment in the early evening that renowned sweet-maker Kishan Lal unpacks his trays of freshly made sev ki barfi, Karachi halwa and samosa; finding the best moong dal halwa in the middle of Old Delhi's gold market; eating a plate of mutton and potato in the shadow of a Mughal arch; watching the comings and goings in a gully that leads to Old Delhi's red light area; sitting quietly at an ancient wooden bench in a chaikhana in Chitli Qabar.

It was a relief, too, to escape the pizza-fication of many of South Delhi's neighbourhoods, to be reminded that I was in a country of vast regional specialities. I hadn't come to India to eat filet-o-fish or spend the afternoon in the air-conditioned food court of a mall.

I occasionally tried to recreate the dishes I found on the streets at home but they were never as good, neither were the 'street food tasting menus' I tried at swanky South Delhi restaurants—and it wasn't just the flies, dust and dirty oil that were missing. Home cooks and even professional chefs can never compete with a street food vendor who's been making the same dish hundreds of times a day, often for decades. Like Baba the baker at All India Fames in Amritsar who has crafted his crispy kulcha for over thirty years. Or the Old and Famous Jalebi Walas in Chandni Chowk who have been piping jalebis to perfection for decades, never deviating from their rhythm, never changing the heat of the stove, never leaving the coils in the bubbling ghee a moment too long.

Some of Old Delhi's most famous dishes, though, come from a very different tradition, as I discovered during an evening trip with one of India's street food experts. That is, when I finally persuaded him to come with me.

Rahul Verma, as street food correspondent for *The Hindu*, has the best job in Indian journalism. It's also perhaps one of the most hazardous. In his quest to bring readers news of the crispest kachoris or definitive biryani, he risks diabetes, hepatitis and high cholesterol. He has pounded the pavements for over twenty years and yet his enthusiasm for the city's street food has never waned. 'When I moved to Delhi,' he once wrote, 'I was like Alice in Wonderland...unlike Alice, the wonders haven't ceased since then.' He's constantly on the trail of recommendations from readers, friends, even his barber, and his greedy delight at finding a new dish is infectious. So much so that his column is the first thing I read on Monday morning and I frequently find myself at whichever joint he has recommended by lunchtime. No establishment is too small or obscure for Rahul; distance and climate seldom deter him. But, he said, when I called him to suggest a trip to Old Delhi, although he'd be happy to meet me, he didn't normally venture into the old city during monsoon.

It was true that glowering skies, intermittent rain and soupy air had turned the summer furnace into a sauna and the slightest exertion was intolerable, but after a few weeks away in Scotland I couldn't wait to get back to discovering new street food dishes and was keen to waste no time meeting this street food guru. I could

Korma, Kheer and Kismet

tell Rahul didn't want to disappoint and he eventually agreed to an outing but warned there would be conditions. 'Meet me in the bar at the Press Club and I'll explain.'

Delhi's Press Club is everything a journalist could wish for—boisterous media types, cheap beer and plentiful snacks. When I arrived, Kingfisher and kakori kebabs were already waiting and Rahul was ready to talk tactics. The only way to deal with Old Delhi at this time of year, he said, is with a plan that goes something like this: 'First,' he warned, 'use plenty of hand sanitizer; germs are breeding in the humidity. Don't touch the fresh chutneys or raw onions—by evening they've been lying around too long in the humidity. Also, keep moving, it's too hot to linger. Most important, be back at the Press Club in time to cool off with more Kingfisher before last orders at 10.30.'

With that, Rahul marched me off to the Central Secretariat Metro station and four stops later we emerged sweatily into Chawri Bazaar where, mindful of our deadline, we took a rickshaw straight to the Jama Masjid. There, even the oppressive damp heat had failed to diminish the area's spirits. Men hurried to and from prayers while women shopped for fabrics and food; motorcyclists weaved in and out and children played in the gullies; bakers pounded dough for bread to feed their burning tandoors; fat men stirred giant cauldrons while the smoky fumes and lapping flames of a hundred kebab stalls beckoned both faithful and faithless.

In the streets around Jama Masjid, every night feels like a special occasion and this is partly because of the food. The small lanes are always packed with vendors and most of the crowds come for the kind of dishes not usually made at home, the indulgent dishes of royal kitchens of the past. 'Mughlai' food, Rahul explained, is more luxurious and extravagant than everyday food. Looking around, it was clear most restaurants and stalls in the area were keen to cash in on their Mughal links, with signs proclaiming their fare 'shahi', 'Mughlai' or even 'Shahjahani'.

My companion, too, was treated like royalty everywhere, with vendors calling out to him and offering him plates of food. Some, I noticed, had laminated copies of his newspaper column pinned to their walls next to garlanded portraits of their ancestors. Our first stop had no royal pretensions or adornment of any kind. In fact, if I hadn't been with Rahul I probably would have missed the spot where a young cook stood behind a brazier in an area not much bigger than a coal bunker, just below street level. 'This stall,' Rahul said, 'was Mian Sa'ab's, although the founder is no more; the young man is his son who has taken over the business.' Swathed in smoke and dripping with sweat, the man expertly juggled dozens of skewers. First, he took handfuls of minced buffalo and packed it around thick skewers. He then took a piece of thread and wound it around the meat. 'This is because,' Rahul told me, 'the meat is so delicate and tender that without the thread, it will fall off the skewer and hence their name, "sutli" kebab.' He then gently laid the freshly packed skewers over the spitting charcoal, making room for them by turning and moving other, almost ready kebabs further along the brazier. When the kebabs on the far right were judged to be perfectly cooked, he lifted the skewers, slid the seared meat on to dried-leaf plates with his bare hands and removed the string. With a quick garnish he handed the plates over to us. He seemed to carry out this assembling, turning, moving and serving simultaneously, both hands moving in a blur. The delicacy of the meat coupled with the ferocity of the spices made for a surprising and delicious few mouthfuls although, in Rahul's view, 'not quite up to his father's standards'.

There was no sign or menu proclaiming royal lineage at Mian Sa'ab's shop but the first Mughal emperor, Babur, would nonetheless have recognized this food as being closely related to the rustic campfire feasts he had enjoyed as a young man when he dined with nomadic shepherds. Babur's kebabs, though, would have been simple, unadorned hunks of sheep's flesh, with nothing of Mian Sa'ab's fiery flavours. This spicing-up of the mild and delicate cuisines the Mughals brought with them became more evident under later rulers. Certainly by the time of Akbar, the royal households were employing Indian as well as Persian and Central Asian cooks in their kitchens, and the robust flavourings, pickles and chutneys provided by the locals produced the dishes we think of as Mughlai today.

Much of what we know about the Mughal style of eating and its legacy comes from the encyclopaedic *Ain-i-Akbari*, a detailed account of the royal household written by one of the third Mughal emperor Akbar's most senior courtiers, Abu'l Fazl. We are told that 'Cooks from all countries prepare a great variety of dishes of all kinds of grains, greens, meat; also oily, sweet and spicy dishes.' Pages are devoted to recipes from the royal kitchen and we learn that the emperor's cooks had to be ready at all times to produce up to a hundred dishes, including khichdi, saag, halwa, pulao, haleem, biryani, dopiaza, dum pukht, kebabs and kheer, accompanied by both chapatti and naan breads. Most of these dishes can still be found on the streets of Old Delhi.

AKBAR'S RECIPES FROM THE *AIN-I-AKBARI*

KABAB

10 seers meat

½ seer ghi

salt, fresh ginger, onions, ¼ seer of each

cuminseed, coriander seed, pepper, cardamums, cloves, 1½ of each

BIRYANI

For a whole Dashmandi sheep, take 2 s. salt; 1 s. ghi; 2 m. saffron, cloves, pepper, cuminseed: it is made in various ways.

A seer is just under 1 kilo, a dam is about 20 grams, a misqal is approximately 6 grams

At our next stop, in a corner of Haveli Azam Khan, we ate one of the classics of Mughlai culinary fusion when Rahul introduced me to 'Mota Biryaniwala', so called because of his physical resemblance to the vast round degh in which he cooks the food that has made him a local legend. The 'Mota' biryani is as robust in taste as its cook is in stature, intensely spiced but clearly closely related to the Persian pilaf.

These two dishes, once served at emperors' tables, would have been more than enough to send me back to the Press Club replete and happy, but apparently they were just appetizers, and we set off next to find somewhere to sit down for dinner. I assumed this meant Karim's, the hundred-year-old restaurant whose owners have built the area's best-known restaurant on claims that their ancestor Mohammed Aziz once worked in the kitchen of the Red Fort for the last Mughal emperor. When the British exiled Bahadur Shah, so their story goes, Aziz was out of a job, but kept the family tradition alive by passing down the royal recipes to his sons, a tradition which has continued to the present day. (Daughters, incidentally, are generally not to be trusted with the secret spice formulas in case they pass on the information to their husbands' families.) Karim's may have been the most successful at marketing their alleged Mughal links but in truth most of the food in the neighbourhood is strongly linked to the Mughal tradition.

That night we ate instead at one of Karim's neighbours, where, Rahul maintained, the food was better. At Jawahar Restaurant, as well as enjoying a tender Mughlai mutton korma, Rahul introduced me to the legacy of another set of invaders. I laughed as we dipped our bread into a plate of 'mutton ishtoo', rich with ghee and spices, a dish which bore about as much resemblance to the watery stews of my childhood as Mota Biryaniwala's did to the pilafs of Persia.

As we were rushing back to the Press Club for last orders, we didn't have time that evening for kulfi, another legacy of the Mughal kitchens. The *Ain-i-Akbari* tells us of the great lengths to which the royal household went to recreate their beloved ices and sherbets when they first came to India. Initially, saltpetre was used as a coolant, which, Abu'l Fazl tells us, 'in gunpowder produces the explosive heat, [but] is used by his Majesty as a means for cooling water, and is thus a source of joy for great and small.' By 1856, saltpetre was replaced by ice and snow brought from the Himalayas via a labour-intensive chain of boats, horses, elephants and men. Today, ice cream flavoured with cardamom, saffron and pistachio is made in exactly the same way as during Akbar's time. Almost every neighbourhood has a kulfi wallah who rings his bell throughout the evening and who, for a few rupees, will pull out a cone from his aluminium moulds packed with ice and salt.

One of Old Delhi's best-known kulfi wallahs is in Sitaram Bazaar, where the Kuremal family have been in business for over a hundred years. From a drab-looking room furnished only with a large chest freezer and a few plastic chairs, the shop sells dozens of flavours of ice cream, many—like fig, pomegranate, tamarind, falsa, blackberry and rose—that hark back to Persian feasts and emperors yearning for home.

The business was started by Pandit Kuremal, who left his ancestral village in Haryana in 1908 at the age of eight to find his fortune in the big city. He learned his trade from an Old Delhi halwai and by the time he was fourteen, had his own pushcart selling two flavours—plain rabri and mango. Over the next forty years, Kuremal built the business into a multi-cart affair. When Pandit's son Mahavir Prasad took over in 1975, he moved the business off the street and into its present shop, tucked in amongst the old havelis of Kucha Pati Ram. Today the family makes over fifty varieties of kulfi and supplies some of South Delhi's swankiest weddings and hotels.

One morning, Mahavir's son Manoj took me to their workshop where I discovered not much had changed since Mughal times. Some workers were sitting on the floor, working their way through mounds of mangoes, others were stirring giant pails of cooling rabri. Manoj told me that the family's main concern is to maintain the quality for which they are renowned. Their milk is still delivered daily from the Hapur Dairy in Uttar Pradesh, they use only the finest fruit and source the best quality nuts— 'Peshawari Pista, lot number 101' to be precise—and saffron from Kashmir. The only thing that had changed since 1908, he said, was the arrival of giant chest freezers for storage. One of the current generation's innovations is one of the family's most delicious ices—stuffed mango kulfi. This is made by removing the stone and some of the flesh of the mango and filling the cavity with rabri. When frozen, the skin is peeled away and the filling sliced to reveal a combination of kulfi and frozen mango flesh.

I had been told by everyone that street food vendors would never part with their recipes so when Manoj happily handed over a couple of family recipes including his grandfather's original for rabri I was surprised and a little smug, and immediately posted the precious details on my blog. Hubris is a terrible thing and readers were quick to point out I'd been had. If the recipe were correct, they said, and the Kuremals really put five grams of saffron costing 450 rupees per gram into five litres of milk, they would be charging a lot more than twenty-five rupees per ice. 'Street food vendors will never part with the actual recipe,' I was told, 'they always leave out or change a key ingredient.'

Rahul Verma, of course, never pesters vendors for recipes and over the years when we've run into each other, he's always mildly, teasingly sceptical about my recipe triumphs. For him, like Alice, the magic is in the wondering.

PANDIT KUREMAL'S KULFI

MAKES 8 SMALL KULFIS

Kulfi is thought to have its origins in the kitchens of the Mughal emperors, when ice was brought daily from the mountains. Traditionally-made kulfi, in earthenware 'barf ki handi' packed with ice and salt, can still be seen all over Old Delhi today, often served with falooda or sweet vermicelli.

INGREDIENTS

   1 litre full cream milk

   80 gms sugar

   Seeds of 2 cardamom pods, ground to a powder

   1 tsp kewra (screwpine essence), or rose water

   Pinch of saffron, ground to a powder

   40 gms ground pistachios

METHOD

To make authentic, cone-shaped kulfi, you will need aluminium moulds with lids, but it can also be made in a plastic tub.

Boil the milk until it is reduced by about half—which will take 30-45 minutes. Stir frequently to avoid burning. Add the sugar and stir until it dissolves. Stir in the ground cardamom seeds, kewra or rosewater, saffron and ground pistachios.

Pour the kulfi mix into a glass bowl then sit the bowl on another bowl filled with ice until the mixture has cooled. Pour the kulfi mixture into the moulds or plastic tub, cover with lids and freeze overnight.

KUREMAL'S FALSA KULFI

'Kulfi' usually refers to ice cream that has been made with thickened milk, but at Kuremal all the ices are referred to as 'kulfi'.

INGREDIENTS

   2 kg falsa berries

   400 gms sugar

   ½ litre water

   2-3 lemons, juiced

   A pinch of chaat masala

METHOD

Crush the falsa berries with the sugar, then stir in the water. Put a fine sieve or muslin cloth over a bowl and tip the falsa mixture into it. Press until all the juice is extracted. Add lemon juice to taste. Pour the falsa juice into kulfi moulds and freeze overnight.

SITA RAM DIWAN CHAND'S CHANA BHATURA

SERVES 6-8

INGREDIENTS

Chana

500 gms chickpeas

1 thumb-sized piece of ginger, peeled and finely chopped

1 cassia leaf

½ tsp bicarbonate of soda

1 tbsp oil or ghee

150 gms chopped onion

100 gms yogurt

100 gms tomatoes, peeled and chopped

½ tsp turmeric

1½ tsp salt

1 tsp ground black pepper

1 heaped tbsp anardana (pomegranate seed) powder

1 tbsp garam masala

½-1 tsp red chilli powder (or to taste)

Spiced Potatoes

2 medium potatoes, with skin on, boiled until cooked

1 tbsp oil

½ onion, finely chopped

1 tomato, peeled and chopped

½ tsp turmeric

½ tsp salt

½ tsp black pepper

¼ tsp red chilli powder

½ tsp anardana powder

1 tsp garam masala

....

METHOD

Soak the chickpeas overnight in cold water. In the morning, drain then put the chickpeas in a large pan with the ginger, cassia leaf, bicarbonate of soda and about 2½ litres of cold water. Boil the chickpeas until they are tender but not mushy, for about 30 minutes.

Meanwhile, in a separate pan, melt the tablespoon of oil or ghee and brown the onions. Add the yogurt, chopped tomatoes and turmeric. Stir well and cook on a low heat until the mixture is a deep reddish brown, then remove from the heat.

When the chickpeas are ready (retain the cooking liquid which will be much reduced) add the onion/tomato mixture and stir well. Add salt, pepper, anardana powder, garam masala and red chilli powder and stir well. Continue cooking until the gravy has thickened, then take off the heat.

To make the spiced potatoes, heat the oil in a pan, add the chopped onion and tomato and cook until browned. Add the turmeric, salt, black pepper, red chilli powder, anardana powder and garam masala to the mix. Cook for a few minutes. Meanwhile, peel the boiled potatoes and chop them into 2-cm cubes. When the spices are roasted, add the potato cubes then stir well to coat them in the spiced mixture. Stir the potato cubes into the chickpea mixture.

Bhatura

Makes 12

150 gms plain flour

150 gms semolina

½ tsp salt

2 tbsp yogurt

150 200 ml water

1 tbsp vegetable oil

Bhatura Stuffing

150 gms paneer, finely chopped

½ tsp salt

½ tsp cumin seeds

½ tsp garam masala

½ tsp ground black pepper

5 gms chopped fresh coriander

METHOD

Mix together the flour, semolina, salt, yogurt and 150 ml of water. Knead well until you have a soft, springy dough. As the flour and semolina absorb the water, you may need to add more water. After about 5 minutes of kneading, you should have a smooth ball of dough. Put the dough in a clean bowl, cover and rest for 4-5 hours.

To make the bhatura stuffing, combine all the ingredients and mix well.

Work a tablespoon of oil into the rested bhatura dough, then divide it into twelve pieces. Roll each piece into a ball between your palms. With your thumb, press a large dent in each ball, put a dessert spoonful of the stuffing into the dent, then close the dough back up over to cover the stuffing. The stuffing should be completely enclosed by the dough.

Roll each stuffed ball out as thinly as possible.

Heat about 6 cm oil in a kadhai. When a small piece of dough dropped into the oil rises quickly to the surface, the oil is the right temperature to fry the bhature. Gently slide in one bhatura, let it cook for a couple of seconds then press it down with a slotted spoon—this helps it to puff up. Flip the bhatura over and press down again. When the bhatura is golden brown and puffed up, remove and drain excess oil. Serve hot.

PICKLED CARROT

The carrots need to be pickled a few days before you want to serve the chana bhatura.

INGREDIENTS

- 200 gms red 'desi' carrots
- 5 gms black mustard seeds
- 1 tsp salt
- ½ tsp turmeric
- Juice of 2 limes
- 250 ml water
- ½ tsp salt
- ¼ tsp red chilli powder

METHOD

Peel and cut the carrot into small batons about ½ cm thick and 6 cm long and place them in a clean and dry jam jar.

Mix together the mustard seed, salt, turmeric, lime juice and water. Pour over the carrot sticks, close the jar and leave the carrots to steep for at least 2 days.

Drain off the pickling liquid, rinse the carrots then mix with ½ teaspoon salt, ¼ teaspoon red chilli and mix well. The carrots are now ready to serve.

TAMARIND SAUCE

INGREDIENTS

> ½ cup tamarind water (made by covering a handful of dried tamarind with warm water then pressing the pulp through a sieve)
>
> 6 tbsp sugar
>
> 1 tsp roasted cumin powder
>
> ½ tsp red chilli powder
>
> ½ tsp salt
>
> ½ tsp garam masala

METHOD

Mix together all the ingredients in a small pan, bring to the boil, then let the mixture bubble for a few minutes until slightly thickened.

Serve with the chickpeas and bhature, pickled carrot and slices of raw onion.

SIX

Sheher

While Anna Hazare and his supporters were very publicly and ostentatiously starving themselves at the Ramlila Maidan and the whole country briefly dared to hope the war on India's corruption was underway, a couple of kilometres away the old city's Muslims were quietly going about the business of fasting for Ramzan. Both groups were managing this in sapping monsoon humidity and daytime temperatures still up in the high thirties.

One evening during Ramzan, I took part in one of Old Delhi's most intensely moving and unforgettable sights—iftar. I arrived as the light was beginning to fade over Jama Masjid, whose first stone was laid by Shah Jahan in 1650, and remains miraculously unscathed by man or time. The muezzin was calling out over the disappearing gullies of Matia Mahal, his voice, as in Ahmed Ali's time, 'rippling with the glory of Islam'. Thousands were clamouring to be inside for the moment the day's fast would end, fighting their way through crowds of hawkers determined to capitalize on a parched and famished crowd with bottled water and fruit. Most, though, in family groups, had brought their own iftar feast with them and pushed through without stopping, trailing scents of heavenly home-made food from giant tiffins.

Eventually over 20,000 people had kicked off their shoes on the steps outside (and would, miraculously, manage to be reunited with them later) and taken their place in the mosque's courtyard. Inside, the scene resembled a giant picnic as women set out plates of meat, rice and fruit on brightly coloured tablecloths and children ran around playing. As the men filed towards the prayer hall and the crowd settled down to wait for the signal to eat, the lights outlining the soaring minarets turned to constellations against the pink, purple then indigo sky.

The atmosphere of unbearable anticipation was eventually punctured by what sounded alarmingly like a series of explosions but was the signal that fasting was over for another day. This was followed by a deep silence and together more than 20,000 people ate and drank for the first time in over twelve hours, an extraordinary reminder of the simplicity and power of faith; enough to make passing doubters feel they might be missing something.

When thirst and hunger had been tamed, whether with a few symbolic dates or something more substantial, the crowds started to make their way out of the mosque. Its steps and the streets below were full of men in new white kurtas, lost in purposeful thought. The lanes were teeming with family groups in their best clothes. Tiny, hand-turned Ferris wheels, still popular during festivals in Old Delhi, had been set up and children were waiting excitedly for their turn. Most took the quickest route to home, restaurant or street food stall. Some would eat their main meal of the day now; others would eat lightly in the evening and take a more substantial meal, known as sehri, just before the start of the next day's fasting. For those who chose to eat out, there was food everywhere—

carts piled with sticky dates, blazing kebab stalls, vast cauldrons of biryani; vendors selling little clay pots of creamy phirni topped with silver leaf, bubbling platters of irresistible shahi tukda—all of which could be washed down with nimbu soda, sweet lassi or the bright red sherbet of Rooh Afza, a traditional cordial made from a blend of fruit, vegetables and herbs. In Al Jawahar restaurant, the larger of the two 'Jawahar' restaurants on the street, there were family groups eating with gusto, dunking pieces of fresh, fluffy tandoori rotis into bowls of korma, and some solitary men sitting apart, devouring kebabs. Shoppers were stocking up on festive specialties like the golden vermicelli which is made into the dish traditionally served at the end of the month's fasting, sheer khurma.

As well as providing Muslims with a period of reflection and introspection, the month's abstinence is also meant to help those fasting empathize with the poor and perpetually hungry. Outside the Rahmatullah Hotel in Matia Mahal there are always dozens of ragged and filthy destitutes—some clearly mentally ill, others deranged from glue-sniffing—the most wretched of India's poor, crouching in lines. They wait patiently for a passing benefactor to buy them a plate of food from the tandoor and the giant pots inside. For a few rupees a man will be given a hearty meal and, during Ramzan, the hungry don't have to wait long.

At the end of Ramzan, on Eid morning, the atmosphere at Jama Masjid is even more magical. I was once lucky enough to watch the Eid prayers from one of its raised chhatris, where I had a panoramic view of the thousands of worshippers inside the mosque and the many more lined up in the lanes and patches of open ground outside. When the prayers began, everyone, inside and outside of the mosque, moved in a single wave. Perched high above the bazaars, it felt as if the soft prayers had the power to silence the city and, as Eid greetings were exchanged all around me, I looked out to Meena Bazaar. The early morning mist seemed to blot out everything beyond the old city, and it was as if, for a few moments there was, once again, nothing but sheher*.

But this Eid I was to celebrate with two residents of 'sheher' who had entered our lives when we were at our lowest ebb and had managed to restore our faith in Delhi landlords and a lot more besides.

We had first met them when we decided our happiness and sanity depended on escaping 'The Bitter End' farmhouse. We were lucky enough to find an atmospheric old house in Nizamuddin West complete with a purdah room and rooftop view of the Mughal splendour of Humayun's Tomb. The owner, Mr Zahoor,

---

*'Sheher', meaning 'city', is the name for Old Delhi still sometimes used by older residents and refers to the time when the walled city was the only city and what lay beyond the walls was nothing but jungle.

and his friend Mr Naseem, met us there one wintry morning when cold winds were whistling through the house's glass-free window frames, contractors were still sanding the mosaic floors, bathrooms were leaking, the kitchen units were being eaten by termites and there was a thick layer of rubble everywhere. In light of our previous problems with landlords, it seemed premature to be agreeing to hand over three months' rent, but in the corner of what would someday presumably be the lounge, Mr Zahoor, Mr Naseem and their various offspring were perched on plastic chairs looking expectantly at us.

As we entered, Mr Naseem rose to his feet and we took a moment to absorb the impact. He was an imposing, upright figure. From the neck down he looked every bit the retired military gent—double-breasted navy blazer with brass buttons, silk cravat, grey slacks, and shiny shoes. His hair, though, seemed to belong somewhere else—on Donald Trump's head, perhaps. It was a triumph of comb-over ingenuity—well-spaced strands of hair had been grown long, hennaed, teased, looped, swirled and folded into a startling bright orange approximation of a full head of hair. While Mr Zahoor sat quietly, swaddled in a tweed waistcoat, muffler and bobble hat, Mr Naseem threw open his arms and began to speak in the rhythms of an Urdu poet addressing an auditorium, 'Oh, Mr Nelson! Zahoor wishes only to convey that, as of this very moment, you are as a brother to him.' At this, Mr Zahoor signalled to a servant and a giant metal tiffin tin was brought in. As Mr Naseem's couplets flowed, 'From our home to yours, with the blessings of our children on your children…' Mr Zahoor opened each of the layers to reveal korma, biryani, naan, shahi tukda and kheer, as well as a large box of sweets from our favourite shop, Chaina Ram. With that, we happily signed the contract. A Zahoor/Naseem delegation was waiting for us when we moved

Korma, Kheer and Kismet

in a few weeks later. Throughout our two-year stay, every rent day, high day and holiday, even the day we all trooped off to Mehrauli to pay the stamp duty on the rent, was marked by the delivery of an Old Delhi feast and an accompanying ode to our kinship.

On Eid morning there was a lull in the monsoon rains and the day was stiflingly hot when we arrived in Old Delhi. We parked the car next to three street children licking smears of curd from scraps of newspaper and waited for one of Mr Naseem's sons to come and find us. He led us through the markets of Bara Hindu Rao where crowds in bright new clothes were returning from the eidgah, buying food and gifts and starting their rounds of family visits.

He has never mentioned it but I wouldn't be surprised to learn that Mr Naseem has Mughal forebears. When we arrived at his home in the backstreets, we found the beaming patriarch dressed in his best kurta, managing to imbue the plastic chair on which he was seated with throne-like qualities. The room, with its pink walls, yellow and pink plastic flowers and chains of fairy lights hanging from the ceiling bathed him in a rosy glow. The pinkness of the room only enhanced his orange hair, which was faring badly in the humidity. A whirring fan was wreaking havoc on the carefully arranged, hennaed strands; every so often an entire flap of hair at the back of his head would rise then slap back down. Eventually, it refused to resume its correct position and fell, moist and lifeless, on his shoulder.

He rose to greet us and was clearly on top form, 'It is our great pleasure that you people take your sacred steps at our home,' he began, then sat us down and immediately laid out an Eid feast for us. First came plates of creamy sheer khurma. He had made the dish himself, he told us, and held out his hand to show blisters from hours of stirring. As soon as it was ready, he said, he had sent one batch to his sister's home and one to Mr Zahoor, his oldest friend.

The two men had met, he told us, when they were students at The Delhi College, both studying English, History, Hindi and Persian. We were surprised to hear that Mr Zahoor had studied English, as we had never heard him utter more than a couple of words in the language, leaving all communication to Mr Naseem. 'Actually, he was not concentrating on the studies,' Mr Naseem explained. 'He was more involved in the student union elections.' After university, the two men went into business. Both started small—Mr Zahoor with keychains, Mr Naseem with locks. Mr Zahoor quickly diversified and built a substantial enterprise. 'He met someone who was doing business in suitcases and briefcases. He joined with him and started learning this work. They opened a big factory to manufacture briefcases and suitcases, manufacturing about 5,000 pieces daily—Ideal Luggage Company. They still have the same name and have one shop in Chandni Chowk and one in Meena Bazaar. They don't manufacture any more, only retailing. He has a godown near Karim's and a cloth shop in Matia Mahal.'

When I asked Mr Naseem about his own business, he handed me a card which read 'Naseemuddin, Lucky Store, Gali Peti Wali, Sadar Bazaar, Wholesale Dealer of cutlery items, nail cutter, tester, locks, pillars, scissors, rat trap, churis, knifes, screw drivers, raisers etc.', then returned to the more urgent matter of filling our stomachs. 'Do not is-stop your hand!' he commanded. In fact our hands were working overtime with crisp kachoris, spicy keema and a vast selection of sweets, which of course had been brought from Chaina Ram in Fatehpuri. When I listened later to the recording I'd made, I realized I was quite happy to sit back and enjoy the delicious food and let Mr Naseem expound on his trade philosophy in the manner of a great emperor addressing his subjects. He became particularly animated when talking about the recent arrival of Chinese products in Sadar Bazaar. 'China is now becoming very famous in the market, pushing in the market of India. And then, what I observe, their quality is nice, it looks nice. Whether it works or not, this is another thing...'

Mr Naseem broke off from his speech-making only to press more food on us. 'It's delicious,' I said, cramming more in my mouth, 'but I really can't eat another thing...' 'Delicious!' he thundered. 'Delicious is when you are taking more. Please take this, I'm sure you will feel that it is very tasty, it is called kalakand from Haldiram's.' Mr Haldiram, he eulogized, certainly knows how to run a successful business. 'He always has a great number of customers—like he might be distributing free of cost.'

Eid is a time of gratitude and reflection and Mr Naseem was in an expansive mood. He gave thanks for his and Mr Zahoor's good fortune but lamented the lot of Muslims in general. He was grateful he had been able to provide for his family; his children had been well-educated and were pursuing good careers. He spoke particularly of his pride in his wife who, over the years, had risen to become a senior nursing superintendent at a hospital in Daryaganj. He knew, though, that most Muslims were not as fortunate, facing severe discrimination, particularly in education, and cited the example of one of Mr Zahoor's daughters. 'We are the most neglected community in India. Our government says that it is very essential for everyone to get the education but if you go deep to touch the reality, you will find big differences. Even the daughter of Zahoor, her marks was more than 90 per cent but she was failed to clear the entrance test.'

A long call to prayer from a nearby mosque was our cue to let Mr Naseem resume his Eid duties, a three-day round of visiting and receiving family. We left him literally 'in the pink' and not just from the glow of his walls. His eyes were twinkling, brimming with love and pride for his wife and children. As we left, he showered us with blessings, wishing us as much good fortune as he had been lucky enough to enjoy. He also promised me the recipe for his wonderful sheer khurma.

A few weeks later, when I called Mr Naseem to remind him about the recipe, I was shocked to find him in uncharacteristically low spirits. Something terrible had happened, he said. His wife had died suddenly and unexpectedly a few days earlier, soon after the birth of the couple's first grandson. In fact, the family was still celebrating when she contracted bronchitis.

A few days later, Dean and I went to visit him at his shop in Peti Wali Gali to pay our respects. He looked like a balloon that had been popped as he told us how his wife had rapidly become critically ill and of his desperate attempts to save her. 'Eventually we persuaded her to go to hospital but day by day her condition was deteriorating. I told them, "I will give 1 lakh, 5 lakh, 100 lakh for saving my wife. Whatever the treatment, give her, because her life is most important for me."' But Mr Naseem was forced to look on helplessly as the treatment failed, his wife slipped away and eventually the machines that were monitoring her fell silent. 'As I was watching, her heart beating became zero.' Now, he said, he was in total despair. His wife was his world, he said, the two of them used to speak on the phone constantly. 'Every minute she was calling me. Now no call is coming. Who will call?'

Working in the shop was the only thing that was keeping him going, he said, but he doubted he would ever recover from the loss of his wife. 'Everything now I feel is completely destroyed. She was my wife, so it was the biggest loss for me. I hear of people who are remarried within a month of their wife is expired—I hate very much. It means her value was only for few days; you are going to forget. I cannot forget.' He nonetheless insisted that we eat and sent

Korma, Kheer and Kismet

out for that ultimate comfort food—chhole bhature.

I called Mr Naseem the following Ramzan to see if we could come and visit him on Eid, but he told me sadly that he wouldn't be celebrating Eid this year and therefore would not be receiving visitors. The larger-than-life character we'd known and loved was gone but he remembered that I had wanted the recipe for his sheer khurma. In a slow monotone, with none of his customary linguistic flourishes, he read it out over the phone:

'Take two kg milk and boil it with four hundred grams rice [the rice is to be ground to powder]. Stir it completely to absorb the milk. It will take one hour or more, keep stirring. When you think rice is completely absorbed, add half kg almonds, cashews, chironji, magaz, cardamom, dates. Cook for half an hour. It will thicken. This is hard work, you have not to stop your hand.'

MR NASEEM'S SHEER KHURMA

SERVES 6

Mr Naseem's sheer khurma was quite runny so I didn't reduce the milk for as long as he stipulated. I may also have misheard the quantity of rice so while testing the recipe, I reduced that too. Vermicelli, which is sold in huge piles all over Old Delhi during Ramzan, is often used instead of ground rice to make khurma. In fact that's the way Mr Zahoor served his on Eid. Different combinations of dried fruit and nuts can be added to the sheer khurma but it's important to include dates as they are the traditional fast-breaking food.

INGREDIENTS

- 1 litre full cream milk
- 20 gms rice, ground to a powder
- 100 gms sugar
- 100 gms of a combination of chopped, pitted dates, chopped almonds, chopped cashews, chironji and magaz (watermelon seeds)
- Pinch of cardamom powder
- A splash of kewra or rosewater

METHOD

Heat the milk and ground rice to boiling point then reduce the heat and let the mixture thicken slightly for about 10-15 minutes. Add the sugar and stir to dissolve then add the dates, almonds, cashews, chironji, magaz, cardamom and kewra or rosewater. Cook a little longer until the sheer khurma is the consistency of thick cream.

SEVEN

Shakarkandi in Ballimaran

The monsoon had done its best and worst. By the end of September, the skies had been washed blue and the colour green had popped back into our lives—foliage desiccated by dust and drought for most of the year now gleamed with vitality; parks, roundabouts, verges, even cracks in the pavement briefly sprouted new growth. Heavy rains had guaranteed the farmers' crops for another year but the city's drainage system had buckled under the annual deluge and the roads bore the scars. Much of Old Delhi resembled a major archaeological excavation site, into which rickshaw wallahs and cart pullers frequently toppled. The streets would stay this way, according to residents, until the next round of local elections when politicians would suddenly be in a hurry to take an interest in the area's infrastructure.

Although it was still warm and humid, there were signs that cooler days were on the way. The incessant hum and drip of air conditioners—the droning soundtrack to our summer—faded, allowing the sights, sounds and smells of our neighbourhood to press back in. I realized that for the last six months I had been living with the volume turned off, without the sweet racket of bulbuls in the trees that shade our roof terrace; without the call of the muezzin from the mosque on the corner or the tinkling bells of a neighbour's early morning puja. I had missed the wafts of singed rotis, and the elderly couple next door, who pottered about on the roof next door listening to All India Radio. I was dismayed, though, to discover that their son seemed to have developed a taste for all-night sessions of Hindi Prog-Rock. And sadly, the tubby, stubbly men in baggy grey vests in the houses opposite were still walking up and down scratching their bellies as I ventured out again to drink my morning tea on the terrace.

It was the calm before the storm of the later autumn festivals—Raksha Bandhan, Janmashtami, Ramzan, Independence Day, Eid had already whizzed past but there were still a few weeks before Navratri, Dussehra and Diwali so there was nothing specific for me to focus on. It was also a melancholy time in our family as our eldest son had just left to go back to Scotland for university and we were struggling to adapt to our emptying nest. So one day when climatic and narrative peace prevailed—I turned to Old Delhi, as I often have, for refuge and comfort and decided to just walk aimlessly.

I don't know if Delhi has ever been a destination of choice for the 'flâneur'—the nineteenth-century urban gentleman described by Charles Baudelaire as 'a person who walks the city in order to experience it'—but in the twenty-first century, recreational walking is not a popular activity in the city. Despite boasting some of the world's most beautiful parks and monuments, the Delhi authorities seem to do everything in their power to discourage walking. Pavements are dirty, cracked or non-existent and invariably colonized by cars, trucks and homeless families, rendering walking a potentially hazardous activity, widely viewed as something you only do if you have no other option. Having discovered other cities I've lived in by taking to the streets, early attempts to explore our first South Delhi neighbourhood came as a shock. As I've mentioned earlier in the book, every time we walked the short distance to the local shops, we were stared at and greeted with perplexed expressions as people helpfully suggested we might like to hire a driver, or at the very least, a maid.

Slowly, I resigned myself to going everywhere by car but I was, for a short while, inspired to give walking one last go by a book called *Delhi: Adventures in a Megacity*, whose author, Sam Miller, set out to walk from Connaught Place in a spiral as far as Gurgaon and Noida. Following an open-air concert in Nehru Park one evening, I decided I would walk slowly back home to Nizamuddin through the wide leafy streets of Lutyens' Delhi, savouring the splendid bungalows and blooming roundabouts. I lasted about fifteen minutes, unnerved by constant comments and staring, impeded by autorickshaw wallahs coming to a halt right in front of me, hoping for a lucrative 'foreigner' fare. I finally gave up just beyond the prime minister's house on Race Course Road when a group of traffic police, with much waving of arms and blowing of whistles, pleaded with me to stop, 'Madam, please, please, why are you walking?' before flagging down a rickshaw and virtually bundling me into it.

In Old Delhi, too, walking is clearly a potentially hazardous occupation—there's always a chance of being mown down by a handcart or runaway bullock and I've often wondered if I would meet my maker as a result of a hurtling, out-of-control porter. It would certainly be difficult to take a turtle for a walk as the flâneurs did but I think Baudelaire might still find it an ideal location in which to 'rejoice in his incognito'. The overriding focus and purpose of Old Delhi, as North India's largest wholesale market, is commerce, and nothing can detract from that. No one is interested in wide-eyed tourists when there are fortunes to be made or lost on jewellery, saris, wedding invitations, spices, election pamphlets and bathroom taps. Generally, a visitor is treated respectfully, politely and, unlike in the tourist traps of Connaught Place and Paharganj, rarely hassled to buy anything; shopkeepers rightly assume that most tourists have no use for an industrial-sized meat mincer or a top-of-the-range Hindware cistern. The food vendors long ago decided that most visitors are too terrified of contracting 'Delhi Belly' to eat anything, but if you do they'll be delighted and you can be sure there will be no 'tourist rates'—you will be charged exactly the same as a day labourer. In the grand Old Delhi scheme of things, you are small fry, an inconsequential by-product of what *you* perceive to be picturesque, exotic, mind-boggling but for those who live and work there, it's just…well, life. And life—even if it involves gasp-worthy ropes of overhead wiring, a jaw-dropping use of every square millimetre of space and the remains of long-gone empires—just has to be got on with, gawping tourists or not. This, I have found, makes for the perfect setting in which to walk and lose yourself.

And so one early autumn morning I set out, as Baudelaire urged, to walk for no other reason than to walk.

When I started out that day, the early market in Naya Bans was still in full swing, the streets a sea of seasonal fruit and vegetables.

Korma, Kheer and Kismet

'Glut' is one of my favourite food words—it takes me back to childhood summers when our kitchen was full of freshly picked, sweet raspberries, too many to eat and needing to be made into jam quickly before their moment passed. Or tomatoes, bursting with flavour as they closed the curtain on summer; or the new season of potatoes, or the fleeting visit of asparagus. In Britain, though, there is now an obsession with offering consumers 'choice'—fruit and vegetables are flown thousands of miles so that we can have strawberries in winter and parsnips in summer. We've lost the excitement of brief abundances and the simple joy of eating a piece of fruit picked at the moment of its own unique perfection.

I may be the only expat in Delhi who doesn't miss supermarkets. Although it did take a little while to adjust, once I'd got over the initial shock of not being able to do all my food shopping in one place, I began to appreciate a return to a more traditional way. In particular, I love that produce is still seasonal and I never tire of seeing the sabzi wallahs in the morning—a young man and his son who arrive every day from their farm on the outskirts of the city on a horse and cart. The spinach shines bright on winter mornings; the first red carrots mean we'll soon be eating gajar ka halwa; lauki tells me it's monsoon time; the heady scent of overripe mangoes that we're at the height of summer.

That morning I noted that the jamun, a fruit that looks like a bloated black olive, had almost disappeared for another year and I still hadn't learned to love it. In Delhi there is always a huge glut of jamuns during the summer as it was one of the trees chosen by the 1912 Town Planning Committee to create 'a sea of foliage' in the new city. Every year the authorities auction off the foraging rights to the trees and one of the distinctive sights of Delhi summers is the purple-splattered pavements of the fruit the foragers missed. Described by food writer Vikram Doctor as 'the essence of the subcontinent's hard soils and searing summers', and prized for its medicinal properties, the jamun is not to everyone's taste. Many find its astringency, which is often enhanced by the addition of salt and spices and can suck the mouth dry, difficult to embrace and often pronounce the jamun, as the Mughal Emperor Babur is said to have done, 'not very good'. I'll stick with the sweet shop variety—'gulab jamun'.

The lychees and musk melons too had already gone and the last few bloated safeda mangoes, ripe to the point of fermenting, were being edged out by the new crop of apples and pears from the Himalayas. As in the rest of the world, some traditional fruits and vegetables are being lost in India, replaced by imported year-round produce from Thailand, America and New Zealand. But in Old Delhi everything you see on the carts is still local and in season, many varieties of fruit and vegetable rarely seen even a couple of kilometres away in South Delhi. The stalls at the corner of Khari Baoli and Church Mission Road are like a weather vane of seasonality where a row of women in brightly coloured saris, using their pallus for shade, sell small amounts of whatever they've picked that morning. Depending on the time of year, that could be delicate purple and white mulberries, khirni (a small yellow berry), falsa (a berry which looks like a reddish blueberry), fresh almonds, a fruit that I never remember the name of which looks like a miniature pomegranate, as well as a whole range of green leaves. These fruits and vegetables will no doubt start to disappear as the children of the foragers head to Gurgaon to work in call centres. In our South Delhi neighbourhood, for instance, there is no longer anyone to pick the fruit of the mulberry tree opposite our house and most of the delicate berries end up as a purple shadow underneath. For now though, Old Delhi continues to remind us of the earth turning rather than food miles travelled.

Most of the shoppers in the morning market were men; sons, brothers, uncles dispatched for the day's supplies but there were also more women on the streets than at other times of the day—mothers and grannies in burqas and saris poking and prodding cucumbers and aubergines, insisting on a first-hand inspection of quality and price. Most of the carts sell only one or two items and shoppers moved from one to the next, haggling and gossiping as they went. By 10.30, the fruit and vegetable vendors started to yield to the street's main business—the shops selling tandoors, giant cooking pots and utensils, kulfi-making equipment, paan leaves and candles—and were starting to sell off the last of the day's stock and head home. In an area where space is at such a premium and even the small gap between buildings can be turned into a profitable 'shop', most of the bazaars have several shifts. In some areas, the difference between the day and night-time trades is enormous. The forlorn stretch between Khari Baoli and Ajmeri Gate, for instance, is by day a wholesale sanitary-ware market and by night the capital's seediest red light district, GB Road. I paused at the corner of Gali Qasim Jan and Lal Kuan, near a butcher's shop where, by the evening, hundreds of excited diners would wait in line for Ustad Moinuddin's wonderful beef kebabs.

As I turned into Gali Qasim Jan it seemed that everyone was taking their time with errands, and, like me, relishing being outdoors again. There was a huddle of women chatting outside one of the dyer's shops, standing around the magical pigment box that can match any dupatta to any kurta simply by adding a little of this, a little of that to a murky old oil can of boiling water. Above them hung dozens of newly transformed pieces of fabric, flapping like giant bunting on strings across the gully. Opposite, and conveniently located for the ladies chattering and waiting for their stoles to be dyed, was the 'Fresh Corner' bakery. A group of schoolgirls was huddled inside, giggling and gossiping, putting off going home to chores and homework. Laid out in the glass cabinet were piles of neatly stacked biscuits and pastries. Suddenly, I saw something so familiar that I felt a pang of longing for my own childhood. The label confirmed they were 'macroons', not the brightly coloured sophisticated French variety but the traditional British ones I knew so well, made from desiccated coconut and glacé cherries. The schoolgirls seemed to be in no hurry to make a purchase so I chatted to the shop's owner, Mohammed Israr, who told me his father Faiz Mohammed, a labourer from Uttar Pradesh, set up the bakery in 1975. He said he'd never heard of 'English' macaroons, that these little bites were just something the family had always made. I bought a small newspaper bag of 'macroons' and, on Mohammed's recommendation, one of cumin biscuits and continued on my walk, nibbling as I went.

It is often said that the British left little mark on the cuisine of India, we tend to think the influence was one-way—that Britain is eternally grateful for chicken tikka masala but that no self-respecting Indian would be caught dead eating our insipid fare. I'm not so sure. Look a little more closely and there are traces of influence everywhere. Indians, apart from the Anglo-Indian community, may have been glad to see the back of our overcooked 1940s roast dinners and anaemic vegetables but they refused to let go of our biscuits. In the area where I was walking that day, Ballimaran, there are more than a dozen old-fashioned bakeries, all doing a roaring trade in hundreds of varieties of biscuit. And any kirana store, where most of India does its shopping, would be unrecognizable with anything less than a shelf full of Britannia biscuits, many of which are versions of old-fashioned British favourites like rich tea, bourbon and digestives.

Could Indians imagine life without the 'ishtoo' (stew) and

'shahi tukda', the bread pudding that Rahul Verma had introduced me to? And what about 'dabal roti'? What would they put their aloo tikkis and masala omelettes on? How on earth would they make bread pakora? And surely the itinerant Old Delhi 'Bombay Sandwich' wallah owes something to the great British afternoon tea? Find him in the Katra Neel cloth market at the Fatehpuri end of Chandni Chowk where he moves around with a portable sandwich counter that looks like an old-fashioned clerk's desk, but with a glass front to show his sandwich fillings. The back of the counter folds down for him to assemble sandwiches to order. Whereas the British would have been content with a dainty sliver of cucumber between two tiny triangles of bread, here, the sandwich wallah smears his two slices of white bread with a spicy green chutney, then builds up layers of sliced potatoes, tomatoes, cucumber, onions and paneer to create a great feast of a sandwich. He then sprinkles the whole lot with a special masala and adds a sachet of ketchup for good measure. He does, though, cut the sandwich into triangles and remove the crusts—British style.

One of Old Delhi's most surprising and unusual street food joints also unwittingly pays homage to the dainty cucumber sandwich. The Jain Coffee House in Raghu Ganj always amazes visitors, partly because of its location, a quiet little grain store tucked away from the mayhem of Chawri Bazaar, but also because of the fresh, sweet delicacy of the fruit sandwiches they serve. The Jain brothers' fare is not for the faint-hearted though, or for anyone who doesn't have a crazy sweet tooth. First a slice of soft white bread is spread generously with orange marmalade. Then layers are built up with butter, slivers of fresh paneer, a handful of sliced grapes, a sprinkling of pomegranate seeds and slices of seasonal fruit—mango in summer and apple in the winter. Then, unless you move quickly to stop him, Mr Jain will sprinkle powdered sugar on top. The family's main business is still grain-trading and the sandwiches are a side line, but what a side line! There's no better way to beat the summer heat and escape busy bazaars—just pull up a sack of grain to sit on, order a chikoo milkshake on the side and tuck in.

During a previous morning ramble, along Chitli Qabar near the Jama Masjid, I discovered the tiny Diamond Bakery whose bakers make nothing but what looks like British-style bread in a coal-fired oven inches from the street. I watched the men at work baking rack after rack of perfect loaves and chatted to the young proprietor who confirmed that the shop had been around since British times. Overcome with longing by the yeasty smell, I asked to buy one. The owner told me this wasn't possible as the bread wasn't ready yet. I was puzzled, wondering how much more ready it could get—well-risen, nicely browned, warm and waiting to be sliced and gobbled down with melting butter. The owner pointed to activity in another corner of the shop. I was astonished to see a group of men slicing up fresh, cooled loaves and putting the slices back in the oven. I realized that the Diamond Bakery loaf exists mainly as a means of producing bags of 'rusks' for dipping in chai, like giant street biscotti. I managed to persuade the owner to sell me a couple of the fresh, 'unready' loaves, which were delicious. It strikes me now that even the rusks are probably a British legacy—a way our thrifty mothers and grandmothers used up stale bread—they just didn't forfeit the pleasure of freshly baked loaves in the process.

I also spotted that day a cart with what looked like a pile of miniature pink and white olives—karaunda. These sour berries, as well as being used in traditional medicine, are usually made into pickles. The British, however, in their relentless bid to recreate Basingstoke in Bengal, decided that if they drowned the karaunda

Korma, Kheer and Kismet

in enough thick sugar syrup, they could turn it into a 'glacé cherry'. Even today, many of the glacé cherries found in Indian grocers are the descendants of the berries the British sugared into submission. The tough thorny karaunda bushes were also one of the bushes used by the British to construct a 2,500-mile long 'customs hedge'. The hedge stretched all the way from the Himalayas to Orissa to prevent the smuggling of salt to avoid taxes, which were an important source of income of the East India Company. It was once described in *The Guardian* as 'one of the most grotesque and least well-known achievements of the British in India', but long after the hedge was dismantled, Indians were still enjoying desi 'glacé cherries'.

A little further along on my autumn walk I stopped to watch bhutte wallah Mohammed Sabir slowly roasting fresh ears of corn for an impatient group of little girls with a few rupees to spend. My leisurely pace also meant that just opposite the cheeky girls, I noticed for the first time, in a spot I'd passed a hundred times, an old man, Mohammed Yasin, dressed in white kurta and cap, sitting cross-legged on a cart. Next to him was a box containing dozens of day-old chicks which he was selling for five rupees each. Just before I turned into Ballimaran, I stopped at an old haveli where Ghalib is believed to have lived and which has now been partially renovated. There was very little in the haveli to suggest the great poet had ever lived there apart from a poster listing his favourite foods—shammi kebabs and kadhi.

One of my favourite sights in Old Delhi, perhaps anywhere, are the khomcha wallahs, the men who carry a whole restaurant in the baskets on their heads or in battered tins strapped to their bicycles. As I turned into Ballimaran, I spotted a young man pushing what looked like a whole shop window on the back of his bicycle. The glass case was divided into four sections, each containing a different vegetarian snack, including one resembling a kebab but was, he assured me, made from dal.

Further along Ballimaran, twin namkeen shops guard the entrance to Jogiwara and, like trying to get past the fairytale trolls under the bridge, it's impossible to pass without handing over a few rupees for bags of deep-fried snacks—much of it very good with a post-Old Delhi beer. By now I was carrying a fair amount of shopping so decided to stop for lunch in Maliwara at a busy chowk where a small temple meets sari shops and brocade merchants. Baba Chaat Corner, although I'd never noticed it before, turned out to be no newcomer in the area. Baba and his father before him have been in that spot in Maliwara for over thirty-five years and their chaat is a favourite with mothers and daughters taking a break from the serious business of wedding shopping. I sat on a ledge outside a glittering sari shop as instructed by Baba and nibbled away at a plate of aloo tikki, watching a school bus work its way through the gully. The Cambridge School 'bus' was not much bigger than a doll's house perched on the back of a cycle rickshaw, but inside were miraculously packed a dozen small children. Every now and then the rickshaw wallah hopped off the cycle to unlatch the back door and lift out a child. He stopped at the chowk and set down a small boy—he couldn't have been more than four or five years old—and handed him a satchel from the rack on the roof. The boy, immaculate in pressed blue shorts and red checked shirt, with a name tag and hanky clipped to his pocket, looked minute as he disappeared into the crowd and then into one of the smaller gullies. I wondered how many parents in Edinburgh these days would let a four-year-old walk back alone from the bus stop.

I was reluctant to end my seemingly aimless ramble but just before I turned towards the Metro and back to the India of economic miracles and shopping malls, I saw what I realized I'd been looking for all along—the truest sign, like the swallows of an English spring, that cooler days were on their way. Freed from his summer hibernation, he strode through the gullies, beaming broadly, with a folded bamboo stand over his shoulder and a tray on his head. I spotted the tray first, bobbing above the crowds, its mound of pink, wrinkled roasted sweet potatoes dotted with lemons and kamrak. As he approached, I signalled for him to stop. He put down the stand, swung the tray down on top of it then selected a sweet potato from the hot embers that were keeping it warm. He peeled the potato, cut it in half and chopped flesh the colour of soft winter sunshine into bite-sized chunks, which he then tipped into a small dried-leaf plate, dressed them with lemon juice and a sprinkling of chaat masala and, with an expert flick of his wrist, mixed the whole lot together before handing it to me.

With a few stabs of the toothpick, the tapas-sized twenty-rupee portion was gone, every smoky, sweet, sour, spicy mouthful devoured greedily. Shakarkandi is one of Old Delhi's healthiest snacks and yet even without ghee, sugar, salt or the slightest contact with a vat of bubbling oil, it manages to taste both comforting and indulgent. Suddenly my mental food calendar clicked over to a new season and I was looking forward to bolstering winter dishes—the pies and stews which I would make at home over the next few months, as well as the street food—the kebabs and aloo tikkis—I would eat, and the recipes I'd write down.

By December, sweet potatoes would be ubiquitous, piled high on carts all over the old city. Then, as temperatures plummet, their role in Old Delhi is more straightforwardly sustaining; they're devoured by shivering labourers and traders or parcelled up by the dozen and carried back to homes in every gully to warm up cold bones.

But for now that first soft sweet mouthful was a reminder that if the mango is God's way of helping us endure the Indian summer, the shakarkandi is our reward for surviving it.

ROASTED SWEET POTATO OR SHAKARKANDI

SERVES 2

Sweet potato roasted at home will never be as good as the perfect little dish prepared by the first shakarkandi wallah of autumn, but it's still very good and especially welcome on a cold afternoon when dinner seems a distant prospect.

INGREDIENTS

    2 medium sweet potatoes
    1 star fruit (kamrak), sliced thinly

1 lemon

Chaat masala to taste

....

METHOD

Preheat the oven to 200°C. Pierce the sweet potatoes a few times so that they don't explode in the oven. Roast for about 30–45 minutes—they should feel soft but not mushy when pierced with a knife. Peel the sweet potatoes, dice into 2 cm pieces, sprinkle with chaat masala and lemon juice. Garnish with slices of star fruit.

EIGHT

Fasting and Feasting

Old Delhi was ready to eat its way from one festival to the next and it was up to the Navratri to get the autumn party started. From the platters of dried fruit, nuts and sweets offered to the gods during the season's numerous pujas, to the giant temporary street canteens that spring up to serve free food to the poor; from the nostalgic neon pink of candyfloss at the Ramlila parade to little plates of 'roller' ice cream at Dussehra; from the frugality of steamed chickpeas and puri during the Navratri to the diabetes-inducing excess of Diwali, food was everywhere and the expanding waistline I was sporting by December was proof I refused nothing.

Unlike Eid, the Navratri are a time of avoidance of certain foods rather than complete abstinence and while there is an emphasis on purification and cleansing, food is still at the heart of the celebrations. Home cooks and restaurant chefs deploy considerable creativity to devise inventive 'vrat ka khana', and there is a wide range of new dishes and snacks to explore. It is a time when, traditionally, stocks of wheat flour are running low just before the harvest, and are replaced by those made from dried singhara, buckwheat, millet and amaranth, resulting in a range of unusual breads. Halwa is made from sweet potato and lauki instead of semolina and tapioca, which I'd last seen in school dinners, is used in a hundred different ways, including in pakoras, fritters and khichdi. I was also delighted to discover that deep-fried snacks, sticky sweets, ghee and milk are still very much on the Navratri menu. Definitely my kind of fast.

I kicked off the season of feasts great and small on the first day of the Navratri in an appropriately restrained but sustaining manner with one of my favourite Old Delhi breakfasts—bedmi aloo and nagori halwa at Ram Swaroop's little shop in Sitaram Bazaar. Then food writer Anoothi Vishal introduced me to a special fasting milk pudding which helped solve the mystery of what I'd initially thought were sacks of polystyrene in the Khari Baoli spice market, but are in fact puffed lotus seeds used for, among other things, 'Indian popcorn' and 'makhane ki kheer'.

My flirtation with fasting lasted until the last few days of the Navratri when the Durga Puja unexpectedly provided one of the food highlights of the season. For most people, the main attraction of the puja is admiring the fabulous pandals which go up in Bengali neighbourhoods. Particularly in Kolkata, the pandals become more elaborate every year; recent creations have included giant replicas of the Taj Mahal, the Tata Nano factory and even Harry Potter's Hogwarts, complete with steam train. The main Bengali area of Delhi, Chittaranjan Park, also celebrates in grand style; craftsmen work for months, moulding and painting elaborate statues of the goddess Durga, and during the puja the streets teem with visitors who wander through the streets, pandal-hopping. But the city's oldest celebration, the Kashmere Gate Durga Puja, takes place in Old Delhi, dating back to 1911 when many Bengalis came to the city to work for the British after the government moved its base from Calcutta. The puja started life in the heart of Old Delhi, in Nai Sarak, then Fatehpuri, before settling in its current home on the lawns of the Bengali Senior Secondary School on Alipur Road.

The eve of the puja is known as the Anand Mela, when local women cook up a storm and bring a selection of their favourite dishes to share with the community. For those more greedy than spiritual, like myself, it is an opportunity to eat their way around Bengali home cooking. I arrived with my Bengali friend Surya and her husband Sean as devotees were pouring into the pandal to the sound of Tagore's beautiful Rabindra Sangeet and being whirled into dance by the dhaki drummers. We dutifully paid our respects to the giant Goddess, a dignified and ornate but, I was told, comparatively low-key idol about twenty feet high, complete with ten arms, each clutching a weapon. Sitting astride a lion, she was accompanied by her four children—Ganesh, Kartikeya, Lakshmi and Saraswati—and looked all set for her annual battle with the evil buffalo god Mahishasura.

With the help of the occasional fact-checking phone call to her mum in Siliguri, a small city in West Bengal, Surya provided me with some of the background to the Durga Puja. The panjika, or Hindu almanac, plays a vital role, she said—as well as giving the dates for festivals and auspicious times for weddings, new business and travel, it also states which mode of transport Durga will choose for her annual earthly visit. This in turn gives followers an indication of what's in store for them in the coming year. Everyone hopes the goddess won't arrive on a horse, for instance, which would augur drought and devastation, or a boat which means floods in the months ahead. Mum in Siliguri was only partially reassuring— while this year Durga would be leaving on an elephant, ensuring a good harvest, she had arrived on a palanquin, meaning famine.

I was distracted from possible future starvation by a commotion in another area of the tent that seemed to signal an imminent feast. Groups of women were ordering men to set out rows of trestle tables, unpacking shopping bags, setting out small stoves, pressure cookers and large plastic tubs. We walked over and watched the women spread neatly embroidered tablecloths and handwritten signs announcing the unfamiliar (to me) treats to come.

As the smells from the women's food began to waft across the tent, nostrils twitched and hungry lines began to form. We joined the queue but just as we were all set to dive in, members of the organizing committee moved in to hold us back in favour of a group of visiting VIPs who had to be felicitated at great length and shown every display in agonizing detail. Eventually the VIPs were safely tucked away in a roped-off enclosure and we were free to push through the crowds and eat. We held out our plates repeatedly to beaming women proudly serving up their family specialities— evocatively named dishes like 'luchi cholar', delicious deep-fried bread and dal; 'jimikand (yam) cutlets'; 'bonanza chilli chicken', 'rashmoni (surprise) kheer'; 'patishapta', pancakes stuffed with coconut; and neat rows of a milky sweet called sandesh. I often think there's no surer sign that you're about to eat well than a table covered in Tupperware, containing lovingly made home-cooked food. And that evening, in a season crammed with feasts, the little plastic boxes full of big treats didn't disappoint. There could have been no better start to the glorious Delhi eating season than the Anand Mela.

The following night, I gave my stomach a rest and went to watch the Ramlila Sawari, an Old Delhi tradition that dates back to the rule of the last Mughal Emperor Bahadur Shah in the nineteenth century. In its heyday, the parade was one of the most important events in the Old Delhi calendar when thousands would throng the streets every evening in the run-up to Dussehra to watch a procession of floats accompanied by elephants, horses, camels and marching bands, and cheer on the characters who take part in the annual epic depiction of the triumph of good over evil. Then, the procession was more than a kilometre long and passed through the whole of the old city, including the Red Fort. In recent years, as the Sawari's wealthier patrons have started to move away from the area, the parade has struggled to survive. When I arrived in Chawri Bazaar, the streets were nonetheless packed with people lining the route, as Ram, Sita and Lakshman made their way to their final showdown. Children swarmed around vendors selling Hanuman masks, bows and arrows, gorged on bright-pink candyfloss and bobbed up and down trying to catch a glimpse of their favourite hero or villain, oblivious to the rickety, makeshift floats pulled by bullocks instead of elephants, the tableaux and costumes that had seen better days and the lacklustre, almost totally tuneless bands.

If the Sawari procession is a fine Old Delhi tradition in decline, the city's Dussehra celebrations become more outlandish, ostentatious and extravagant every year. For ten days, the Red Fort pales into insignificance as an elaborate stage set, fairground rides and skyscraper-sized effigies of the evil king Ravana, his brother Kumbhakarna and son Meghnad dominate the parade ground in front of it. Scenes from the *Ramayana* are performed nightly in front of enormous crowds, accompanied by mesmerizing pyrotechnics and special effects. Everyone from Manmohan Singh to Sonia Gandhi as well as Bollywood and TV soap stars flock to the Ramlila grounds to make sure evil, in the shape of Ravana, is vanquished for another year.

The food at the Ramlila was, according to the T-shirts worn by the vendors, 'High Class Chaat', and certainly looked impressive on its brightly lit displays. But it was mostly the same dishes available a few yards away in Chandni Chowk but at five times the price. The exception was the giant stand of roller ice cream, an old fashioned novelty which appears only during festivals. It was essentially a six-foot cylinder of ice revolving on a spit. As it turned, the vendor scraped off portions and added slices of banana, mango and pomegranate and drizzles of flavoured cordials. My lasting impression of the night, though, was of the most overwhelming crowd I experienced that year, in fact any year. I had to work very hard to banish thoughts of what might happen if the crowd of many, many thousands all decided to make a dash for the very few exits.

A few days after Ravana had been reduced to ash, Durga had been dunked in the Yamuna, and evil overcome for another year, I took an overnight train to the centre of India to celebrate the mother of all festivals, Diwali, with a family whose roots are in Old Delhi.

The only sign that Old Delhi was ever the centre of India's bidi industry is a small shuttered shop in the Khari Baoli spice market, wedged between one vendor selling Ayurvedic medicine and another whose thriving trade in cardboard boxes spills out on to the pavement in front. The board announcing '207 B.R. and Company 504' is almost obscured by a tangle of thick cables and the shop's entrance is hidden by a paan wallah's stall on the pavement, and I would never have noticed it if I hadn't been taken there by one of the owners of the company, Nita Khanna.

I had known Nita for years before I discovered that her family's bidi company started life in Khari Baoli. As a young man in the 1930s, Nita's grandfather, Chintamanrao Pimplapure, was employed by Cee Jay Company which is now one of the largest bidi companies in India. When Cee Jay refused to promote him, Chintamanrao decided to strike out on his own with two friends, Poonjabhai Patel and Jeorajbhai Patel. The three men stood in Naya Bans, yards from where the Old Delhi office still stands, and scribbled out a partnership agreement on a piece of paper. That Naya Bans agreement later became a crucial piece of evidence in a partnership dispute in the 1950s.

As the business grew, the partners relocated to Sagar, in India's heartland state of Madhya Pradesh, and the Khari Baoli office is now just a repository of old ledgers and memories. These days Nita's main connection with Old Delhi is an annual trip to Faqir Chand, the dried fruit and nut shop in Khari Baoli where her family has always bought the boxes of badam giri and plump Afghan raisins they send out to their customers at Diwali. A few days before Diwali, she invited me along.

Old Delhi reaches fever pitch in the weeks leading up to Diwali and in most of the lanes, it was impossible to move for festive shoppers. Nai Sarak and Kinari Bazaar were under siege

from groups of women trying to decide which sari to buy for which occasion; Dariba Kalan, 'Silver Street', and Kucha Mahajan, Old Delhi's mesmerizing gold market, were virtually buried under the hordes of customers buying up jewellery in industrial quantities; pavements overflowed with stalls selling garish and glittery decorations, and old women from outlying villages waited patiently for sales of their brightly painted clay idols. Everywhere, the chaat wallahs were working overtime to keep up the blood sugar levels of exhausted shoppers. The spice market was choked with people eyeing glittery gift boxes piled on every inch of pavement and shop floor and when we arrived at Faqir Chand, the traders were all bellowing into phones while trying to serve six people simultaneously.

Round the corner, embedded in the walls of the Fatehpuri Mosque, queues stretched into Katra Baryan as a dozen shopkeepers tried to maintain order at Old Delhi's favourite sweet shop, Chaina Ram. The shop's signature sweet is a teeth-sticking Karachi halwa but they have a reputation for all-round excellence, priding themselves on never compromising on the quality of their ingredients, even when demand is so high at Diwali. Others are less scrupulous. Every year during the festive season, the Food and Drug Administration raids hundreds of sweet shops in the city and seizes thousands of kilos of khoya, the milk solids from which many sweets are made and which is often adulterated with milk powder, caustic soda and worse. It struck me that it would be virtually impossible to tell if khoya has been adulterated as it all looks (to me at least) identical. Perhaps that was why, as I read in *The Times of India*, consumers were being offered 'an impurity detection kit'.

I'd actually never heard of khoya until I came to live in India, but as a dairy fan I soon embraced it along with all the other hundreds of ingenious ways Indian cooks use milk. In Old Delhi alone there is a staggering range of street food which relies on milk, from Bade Mian's kheer to the Old and Famous Jalebi Wala, from Natraj's dahi bhallas on the corner of the teeming lane which leads from Chandni Chowk to the metro, to the yogurt that is drizzled over a hundred types of chaat. There's the lassi and faluda

Korma, Kheer and Kismet

at Giani on Church Mission Road and the best mishti doi in Delhi at Annapurna Sweets. And the sweets—from 101 types of barfi to hot platters of gajar ka halwa, from Hazari Lal's khurchan (literally the 'scrapings' of milk which stick to the pan when milk is boiled) to my favourite late afternoon pick-me-up, the milk cake at Hemchand Ladli Prashad's tea stall in Kucha Ghasi Ram.

Of all of the milk products, to me khoya is the most intriguing because it simply doesn't feature in European cooking. When I first saw the round 'cakes' of khoya piled in the shops in Khari Baoli and Church Mission Road, I mistook them for cheeses—but on a visit to Old Delhi's wholesale khoya market I learned some of the intricacies of khoya production. A dusty rickshaw ride away from Old Delhi Railway Station, the Mori Gate khoya market is the wholesale auction site for the tons of milk solids that arrive every day from surrounding states. When I arrived mid-morning, trading was already in full swing and the air was thick with a milky, dairy-parlour sweetness, the traders already unpacking their creamy mounds of khoya wrapped in beautiful old saris for prospective buyers to inspect.

I already knew that khoya is milk that has been reduced to remove the liquid, leaving behind milk solids. But at the khoya market I discovered there are several categories of khoya, graded according to how much liquid has been removed. The softest, which looks like curd cheese, is used for making dishes like gulab jamuns while the firmest, pindi, which looks like whole Cheddar cheeses, are used to make barfi sweets. I decided on the hardest one (the trader asked if I was a halwai!) and was presented with one kilo of beautifully moulded khoya. On the way home I wondered if I should stop and buy an impurity testing kit.

That Diwali, though, I had no need to worry about the adulteration of milk as I left Old Delhi behind and spent a few days with Nita's family in Sagar. At the Pimplapures' beautiful 1960s Madhya Pradesh home, time seems to have stood still. Reading matter in my room included Enid Blyton and copies of *Life* with Jackie Kennedy on the cover; everyone still calls Nita 'Baby'; and the family still has its own dairy at the back of the house. In fact, the first thing we did on arrival was accompany Nita's mother, Meena Pimplapure, to the cowshed for a puja. As she offered ghee to a cow and her calf, she explained that Vasu Baras is always the first—and for rural communities, the most important—of the Diwali ceremonies, when cows are honoured for the food and labour they provide.

For the next few days it was hard to keep up with the pujas and customs. There were days for buying gold and kitchen utensils; there was a lengthy and elaborate Dhanteras puja in front of the family's safe to pray for a prosperous year ahead; Shiv lings were placed in a tulsi plant and the family's old ayah made a cow-dung hillock for the Govardhan puja. There seemed to be a constant tinkling of bells and placing of tilaks on foreheads in the house as the pandit, the third generation to attend to the family, went about his business. To everyone's delight, on Diwali morning he informed us that according to the lunar calendar there would be an extra month of summer in the next twelve months—excellent news for the growing season of the tendu leaves which are used to wrap bidis.

In between official and traditional Diwali duties, there was also plenty of time for what the Pimplapures called 'pet (stomach) puja'. This puja is to me the most sacred, of course, and I was happiest when I was at the centre of its rituals and offerings—the kitchen. The family still runs a traditional Hindu vegetarian kitchen where everything is made from scratch. The daily routine starts early in the morning when several pails of warm milk are brought in from the cows whose enclosure can be seen from the kitchen window.

This is then taken into the dairy area of the kitchen, boiled, then left to settle. The cream that rises to the surface is collected and saved for three days, then turned into the purest white butter, some of which will become ghee. The previous day's milk is made into yogurt to be served at lunchtime. Any leftover yogurt might then be hung for a few hours to make shrikhand for dinner. Meena told me there was once a time when yogurt was made twice a day as her father-in-law and husband refused to eat at dinner any yogurt that had been made in the morning. Surplus milk is turned into the creamiest paneer and khoya.

A little later in the morning, the vegetables arrive from the garden—tomatoes, methi, peas, cauliflower, radishes and ber. Meena then decides, with one of their cooks, Ram Naresh, on the day's menus. By late morning, the cooks are busy chopping, frying and stirring for lunch and two local women come in to make rotis.

During the Diwali period, extra cooks are drafted in to fill tins with festive treats like chakli, a deep-fried savoury snack made from chana dal and rice flour, to which I quickly became addicted and managed to eat at every meal, and karanji, crescent-shaped sweet pastries also known as gujiya, without which, according to Meena, 'there is no festival'. I was itching to watch the cooks in action but before anything could be made, a very special ingredient had to be prepared, one that would be needed for many of the sweet recipes—a dehydrated and powdered sugar called 'bura shakkar'. A cook called Suman took a cup of sugar and a cup of water and heated it as if making 'chaasni', a sugar syrup. She then heated the syrup to remove all the water and sieved the remaining powder. This, she told me, has a much finer texture and better flavour than normal sugar—it also contains less moisture, making it ideal for sweets like laddoos. 'If you make laddoos with normal sugar,' Suman tells me, 'the laddoos will stick in your throat.'

Preparation for Diwali involved days of fiddly, painstaking work and anyone who had a spare few minutes was co-opted. Outside, lights were strung all over the garden and a woman spent a morning making a detailed rangoli on the verandah. In the kitchen, out came the family's old, hand-carved gujiya moulds, pestles and mortars and well-worn chopping boards, all of which had been pounded, patted and pressed by generations of women. I sat on the floor for hours with a group of women as they rolled, stuffed and shaped. Bangles jangled and easy chatter made light work of the detailed, precise, repetitive tasks involved in making Diwali specialities from recipes handed down over generations from mother to daughter.

Meena's daughter-in-law Asha showed me how to make anarsa, a biscuit made from rice flour and deep fried in ghee. Actually, I should say she showed me the final stages of making anarsa as the whole process of making the rice paste takes several days of soaking and fermentation. On another day, Meena came to give us all a master class in making a delicate little pastry called chirote, from a recipe she had learned from her grandmother, Lakshmi Bai Lokar. In those days, Meena told us, the women would get up at 2.30 a.m. on Diwali morning to bathe and oil themselves. Then, she said, festive specialities like chirote and anarsa were always made at home and only eaten on special days; now they're more likely to be factory made and eaten at any time of the year. 'We don't have the excitement of eating special things on special days,' she said. 'People eat them at any time.' We all took turns at rolling, folding and frying the chirote but everyone admitted that no one made them as light, white and crisp as Meena. Nibbling on sweet karanji, anarsa and chirote, made in the laborious, traditional way, hot from the pan in the Pimplapures' kitchen, that Diwali was undoubtedly one of the high spots of my lifetime of greed.

On Diwali morning, the Pimplapures' large drawing room filled with the families of company employees arriving to pay their respects to Meena, Nita and Asha. While the women in their glittering saris sat in little groups on the floor, the Pimplapures sat on chairs at the front of the room. One year, Meena said, she tried to make the proceedings more egalitarian by sitting on the floor with the women but they protested so much she had to sit back on a chair. 'Feudal,' said Nita. 'It's the only way to describe it.'

As the last of the Diwali firecrackers fizzled on the streets of Sagar, the sound of the ticking clock in the Pimplapures' house seemed to grow louder. Even the most bullish members of the family agree that the bidi business is a 'sunset industry' and Meena is concerned about what comes next for her children and grandchildren. She also worries about what will happen to the thousands of people who rely on income from bidi-rolling. 'India's great wealth is its human resources,' she said. 'We will succeed only if we find a way to utilize it wisely, thoughtfully and kindly.'

In Meena's kitchen, change has already come. The younger members of the family, with busy metropolitan lives, don't have time to make complicated and time-consuming recipes like chirote and anarsa. And with only four permanent residents at the Sagar house, a full-time dairy, with dozens of cows and a team of cattle handlers, is no longer needed. But Meena won't be the one to dismantle it. That, she says, is for the next generation. For now, she'll continue to eat yogurt at every meal, fill her cupboards with ghee and give away what's left. And the days when packages of Pimplapure ghee, paneer and khoya find their way to my kitchen in Delhi are very happy days indeed.

MEENA PIMPLAPURE'S CHIROTE

MAKES AT LEAST 24

When I think back to the day I watched a group of women making these traditional Diwali treats, I remember happy hours watching nimble fingers kneading and the sound of soft chatter and bangles jangling; Meena keeping the younger generation in line, ensuring that the family recipe survives unaltered for at least another generation. As well as being a thoroughly enjoyable way to spend an afternoon, I was also reminded that there are few things which connect us to our families, our communities, our roots as powerfully as the food we make.

Don't be fooled by the chirote's humble ingredients and simple techniques though, they require a fair bit of practice to perfect. The dough is fragile to handle and the pounding requires muscle power. But the main pressure point is in the frying: the ghee has to be hot enough to make the chirote crisp but low enough to keep them pale in colour.

Despite filming Meena making chirote and watching the clip umpteen times, toiling over several batches of chirote myself and cooking them at six different temperatures, I have been unable to achieve the ethereal snowy crispness of Meena's chirote. But that's as it should be—in the grand scheme of ancient family recipes, refined and practised over generations, I'm still a complete novice. Meena's chirote were light, crisp and delicately sweet. Mine were just fairly good.

INGREDIENTS

Chirote Dough
350 gms plain flour

80 gms semolina

¼ tsp salt

3 tbsp ghee

250-300 ml warm milk

Paste

2 tbsp ghee mixed with two tbsp rice flour

Ghee for frying the chirote

Icing sugar for dusting

....

METHOD

Mix together the flour, semolina, salt and ghee with your hands then add the milk gradually to form a ball of smooth, firm dough. Cover and leave to rest for 2-3 hours.

Take a lime-sized piece of dough and pound it with a little milk in a pestle and mortar for about 2 minutes until the dough is smooth and soft. Place it on a work surface then roll out to a disc about 20 cm wide then spread a teaspoon of the ghee/rice flour paste all over the surface. Take another lime-sized piece of dough and repeat the process. Lay one disc on top of the other then roll the two discs into a fat sausage. Cut the long roll into six pieces, each piece about 3-4 cm wide. You should now have six pieces roughly 3 cm x 3 cm. Roll each of these into a rectangle/oblong about 9 cm x 9 cm, pressing down more heavily in the centre of the chirote to leave the layers fanning out slightly at the edges.

Heat a few centimetres' depth of ghee in a kadhai. The key to perfectly-fried chirote is in the temperature of the ghee. According to Meena's grandmother, the finished chirote should be almost white. I tried cooking my chirote at six different temperatures. At 160, 150, 140 °C they browned almost immediately. The best result came at about 120 °C (if you don't have a thermometer, then it's all down to trial and error!).

Slide one chirota into the ghee, let it sizzle for a few seconds, then turn it over with a slotted spoon. Then move the chirota to the edge of the pan and tip it on its side so that the exposed layers are facing upwards. Hold it there with the slotted spoon, and with a ladle pour some of the hot ghee through the layers. Do this several times—the layers will open up slightly but don't let the chirota brown. Flip the chirota over so the other end of layers is facing you and ladle the ghee through again. The chirota should be fairly crisp but still pale. Scoop the chirota out of the ghee and let it drain on kitchen roll. Repeat the process until you have used up all the dough.

Chirote are sometimes dipped in syrup before serving and you can give them a modern spin and experiment with flavourings in the syrup. But I like them the way Meena made them, with the lightest dusting of icing sugar over the (hopefully) pale and crisp chirote. The chirote will keep for a few days in a tin.

NINE

Kheer and Kismet

Just a few steps from the Chawri Bazaar metro station in Hauz Qazi Chowk, if you don't mind running the risk of tripping over potholes, going under the wheel of a rickshaw or colliding with a porter, keep looking up and, after a few hundred yards, you'll see a small red mosque which seems to float above bazaar Sirkiwalan. Look down again and pick out a bright green door in the middle of a cluster of hardware shops and go through it. Walk up the steps and at the top you'll find yourself in an open courtyard facing a small, recently restored, red, white and green mosque, which a brightly painted sign identifies as the Masjid Mubarak Begum. As the two courtly caretakers proudly show you around the beautiful, tranquil building, the sights and sounds of the street disappear below your feet, and, before you know it, you'll feel as if you're in a Mughal miniature painting.

The mosque was built in the 1820s by Mubarak Begum, one of the thirteen wives that Sir David Ochterlony, Delhi's first British Resident, is said to have paraded around the city on elephants. According to papers in the Delhi Commissioner's Office, the begum,

Mubarak ul-Nissa, was originally a Brahmin slave girl from Pune who was sold to Ochterlony at the age of twelve. She converted to Islam, became Ochterlony's favourite wife and transformed herself into a powerful Delhi figure in her own right. But she managed to anger both the British and the Mughals by referring to herself as 'Lady Ochterlony' and 'Qudsia Begum'. Despite wielding great influence at the time—one insider of the period noted that 'she is the mistress now of everyone within the walls'—she was an extremely unpopular figure and the mosque she built became known as 'Randi ka Masjid', and no respectable Muslim would set foot in it. Despite the best efforts of the caretakers to restore the Begum's reputation, the mosque is still sometimes referred to by locals as 'The Whore's Mosque'.

A few steps from the mosque, on the opposite side of the street, lies the birthplace of a more universally loved woman, one of India's greatest Bollywood stars, Madhubala. The 'woman of honey' was India's Marilyn Monroe; a woman defined by impossible beauty and nation-gripping sadness; the woman every woman wanted to be and every man wanted to be with, whose short, often tragic life matched the melodrama of the films she starred in. She appeared in her first film at the age of nine and was a leading lady by fourteen; she had a domineering father, an unrequited love and died young of a heart defect. Biographies of the actress often gloss over her early childhood but in fact, Madhubala was born Mumtaz Jahan Begum Dehlavi in 1933, the fifth of eleven children of Ataullah Khan, a low-paid employee of Imperial Tobacco Company, in the heart of Old Delhi. Her carefree childhood in the gullies of the old city was short-lived, though. When she was eight, her father lost his job and moved the family to Bombay where, a year later, she starred in her first film and for the rest of her short life, supported her entire family through her acting.

Korma, Kheer and Kismet

The man who now sits every day in a shop on what was the ground floor of Madhubala's old house, Jamaluddin Siddique, will tell you that it was simply her duty, her destiny, her 'kismet'; just as it was Mubarak Begum's fate to be plucked from slavery, elevated to the highest echelons of society, only to be shunned by the company she found herself in. Jamaluddin Siddique is an owlish, occasionally twinkly-eyed man in a checked lungi who, for up to twelve hours a day, every day, perches behind a large platter containing his own kismet—kheer.

Although I had never really been a rice pudding fan (like many, I never recovered from the British school dinner version), nowadays whenever I go to Old Delhi in the morning, my first stop is nearly always Bade Mian's kheer shop. Their kheer bears no resemblance to the anaemic, lumpy semolina and tapioca I remember from my childhood. First, it boasts a healthy pale caramel colour and the rice has been cooked so slowly, the grains are barely discernible. It's rich, creamy and with a hint of toffee and smoke from the long, slow cooking over a wood fire. In the immortal words of another straight-talking, hitherto rice pudding-loathing friend, 'this tastes frickin' amazing'. Usually I arrive before the kheer so I sit at one of the tables to wait for the day's batch to arrive and watch the family's goat munching on leaves. One of the Siddique brothers brings me chai and chats while I wait to demolish one, sometimes two square metal dishes of what I now consider to be the breakfast of champions—Bade Mian's still-warm, freshly made kheer.

One late autumn morning I sat in the shop with Jamaluddin and his younger brother Abdul Qayyum while they told me about the shop's history. Their great grandfather, Azim Baksh, set up the family kheer business in 1880, about half a century after Mubarak Begum prayed her last across the road and fifty years before Madhubala was born in the rooms above the shop. The family had lived for as long as anyone can remember in the streets around the Hauz Qazi police station. They were originally 'doodh wallahs' who kept a herd of buffaloes but often found themselves with a surplus of milk. 'We used to sell milk but there was still so much of it left over and it wasn't getting used at home.' It was Jamaluddin's grandmother who hit on the idea of making kheer with the surplus milk. 'That's how it started,' he says. 'People would come to buy milk

Korma, Kheer and Kismet

then maybe buy a bit of kheer.' In those days, he told me, kheer used to be prescribed by hakims for upset stomachs. 'Nowadays when you get sick you take medicine or get an injection. Back then, if you were sick, or had a problem in your tummy, they would tell you to eat kheer.'

I asked the brothers the secret of their rice pudding. Jamaluddin's expression went from owlish to twinkly in a heartbeat. 'I can tell you everything!' he beamed. Experience had taught me that this was unlikely but nevertheless I was all ears. The daily routine, he said, hasn't changed for four generations. 'No holidays for us! First of all namaz—early morning prayers at about 5 a.m. Then the milk arrives—it comes from Ghaziabad in UP, pure buffalo milk, nothing else. By 11 a.m., it's made.' I felt sure there was more to it than that but when I started to press for details, the twinkle began to fade. 'Many people have tried to copy our kheer but no one has been able to make it like we have.' But if I really wanted to know the secret, he said, 'It's all from the blessings of Allah.' How many litres did he make every day? I wondered. 'You don't need to worry about that.' Abdul Qayyum helpfully tried to elaborate, 'About sixty litres at least.' His big brother shot him a warning look and tried to wrap up the conversation quickly, 'You get the milk, then that's the process of making kheer,' he said with finality. Sensing my disappointment, Abdul Qayyum again tried to be more forthcoming, 'You put the rice in, then you put the sugar in, you boil it all together.' Whatever then passed between the brothers brought the conversation to an abrupt halt with Jamaluddin only adding that the kheer, since his grandmother's time, had always been made over a wood fire. The last detail he parted with was that the pot must be stirred constantly and that it is his older brother, Mohammed Shafir, who does the stirring. I was surprised, I said, I had always assumed that Jamaluddin was the 'bade mian' as he is the brother everyone associates with the shop. I asked if it would be possible to come and watch the kheer being made one morning but I already knew the answer to my question. 'You'll have to come early in the morning, after prayers.' I said I was happy to come at any time but he was having none of it, 'There's no great secret, make it fresh, sell it fresh, that's it. But it's all made through Allah's blessings.' The owl was back, and I suspected I would wonder forever about the mysterious transubstantiation of milk into kheer that happens every morning between 5 and 11, somewhere near the Hauz Qazi police station.

As the name of Allah increasingly became the answer to all my culinary queries, I realized I was unlikely to make much more headway. But as the brothers batted away my requests for a kheer master class, they perhaps unintentionally revealed a lot more about the personal dramas in their lives. Even during our first conversation that autumn morning, there were clouds gathering around the family and as Jamaluddin went backwards and forwards to serve customers, a more melancholy side to the smiling kheer wallahs began to emerge.

These days, Jamaluddin is reconciled to his role in life but, he told me, it wasn't always so. Now, he said, he's happy to be a 'lungi wallah' but as a boy, he had dreams. One of eight brothers, his earliest memory was going to the cinema with his father to watch films like *Mughal-e-Azam*, a sweeping tale of love, death and heartbreak set in the Mughal era. He remembers listening to his father's stories of the time the film's star, Madhubala, came back to visit her birthplace and drove up and down the street in a limousine. As a young man he set his heart on becoming a wrestler and made good use of the family's milk surplus to build his muscles. 'All I cared about was making a wrestler's body and putting on nice clothes, I didn't worry about anything else. I drank five litres of buffalo milk a day.' Then, he and his brothers started to nag their father, Abdul Rahim, to think big, to diversify, to move on from the crummy hole in the wall in Lal Kuan. Their father, he says, was a simple man and saw things differently. 'If you want a big house and a car, change the work,' he would tell them. 'If you want clothes on your back, if you want to be healthy, if you want roti in your stomach, then stay with this.'

Unlike his heroine, Jamaluddin's destiny has never taken him beyond Hauz Qazi Chowk. For most of his fifty-two years, Jamaluddin Siddique's view of the world has been framed by a narrow doorway on Bazaar Sirkiwalan—the Badal Beg mosque opposite, the clanking of the hardware shops and the constant blur of cycle rickshaws and handcarts. Occasionally the traffic outside the shop is halted when rows of devotees bring the whole teeming street to a halt for namaz. I wondered if he still dreamed of moving further afield. 'Everyone has that in their heart, that they want more than what they have. But in everyone's head is kismet.'

But if Jamaluddin and his brothers have never strayed far from Old Delhi, they often feel as if the world comes to them and they spoke with pride of customers who come from far and wide to enjoy their kheer. Jamaluddin can't imagine ever leaving the shop but still his mind wanders sometimes. So what's next for the brothers and their sons? 'I'm coming to that. Don't be in a hurry. I'm going to tell you something huge—keep it for the end of your book.' Just then, though, a third man, whom I took to be another brother, slid into a seat nearby and Jamaluddin wandered off to serve customers. When he sat back down, the other man leaned over to listen as Jamaluddin began, 'I am a simple man, I have dedicated my whole life to this place. I come here early in the morning and leave late at night, sometimes ten o'clock, sometimes twelve o'clock. My wife says, "You never have time for me." A woman has a heart too, doesn't she? I only have one son; he would like to spend some time with his father. I can't, I'm here.' He stopped and asked me to come outside—he didn't want to say any more in front of the other man, who, it turned out, was not a brother but a nosy dhobi. He pointed to a partition down the middle of the shop. The reason for it, Jamaluddin said, is something that blights Indian businesses from Mukesh and Anil Ambani right down to humble kheer wallahs—sibling rivalry.

'My older brother's wife passed away,' he said. 'In 2001, he married again a woman half his age—he's sixty, she's thirty-five. She married him because of greed, her whole family are greedy people. She manipulated my brother to put the whole shop in his name. Before, it was in our father's name. So he went to the registry and put the whole shop in his name. He then said he wants to split the shop in half and sell one portion. In 2004, they put up the wall and our older brother said he wanted to sell that side but we [he and Abdul] didn't want to sell it, it belonged to our father. But we didn't contest it because we didn't want to ruin our father's reputation.' He then used a beautiful expression to describe the damage his elder brother has done to the family, 'Jhadu ki rassi ko kaatke usne alag alag kar diya saara parivaar.' (He cut the string that bound the broom together and broke the family apart).'The dhobi, not wanting to miss anything, had by now followed us outside. What will happen? I wondered. Jamaluddin forced a twinkle back in his eyes but he looked resigned, 'In every cricket team there are two players who carry the team—that's us two,' he said, pointing at Abdul Qayyum. 'I'm Sachin Tendulkar, he's Rahul Dravid.' With that he was off again to serve customers, but this time he didn't come back, signalling that all conversation about the family schism was over for the day.

A few weeks later, I popped back to see Jamaluddin on the

evening of Eid ul-Adha, or Bakra Eid, the day when the Old City's Muslim families remember Ibrahim's willingness to sacrifice his only son Ishmael. After morning prayers on Eid ul-Adha, Muslim families slaughter a symbolic goat which has been fattened for the purpose, then the meat is shared out between family members and the poor. I was surprised that evening to find the Siddique family's plump goat still munching away behind the counter, somehow having survived the day's rituals. It just wasn't her time for qurbani this year, said Jamaluddin, looking up at the sky.

I was also surprised to see a middle-aged woman dressed in hijab sitting at one of the tables—it's rare to see women in Old Delhi's eateries. She was, Jamaluddin explained, his wife. Abdul Qayyum was also there and the three seemed weary and agitated. Our conversation immediately resumed where Jamaluddin had stopped it on the previous occasion, this time with the additional forceful interventions of his wife. 'We have been telling him to separate the business,' she said, referring to the rift with their elder brother. 'There is nothing left in the partnership.' They had, she said, now even moved out of the home they shared with elder brother Mohammad Shafir. Jamaluddin reached again for more cricketing metaphors, which were largely lost on me, 'Look, when such situations come in life, like in cricket there is one player who is intelligent, one who is a rookie and panics. Mine is a very patient game.' Sensing my lack of nuanced cricket knowledge, he tried kite-flying metaphors, 'If you let it go loose the other person would benefit.' That didn't help either, so he tried Allah, 'When Allah wants that your day will come, you'll forget these days have passed. You should hope for better days from Allah.' But his wife wasn't convinced. 'Responsibility,' she said, 'doesn't mean that a human being doesn't eat his meals, doesn't have his breakfast, doesn't care, doesn't rest a little.' He looked embarrassed by her outburst and tried to change the subject but she wouldn't be stopped. 'If something happens to him, what do I have in this world? I have nothing. My life is with him.' Jamaluddin grew increasingly uncomfortable as she continued. 'He has sacrificed his happiness, his wife's and kid's happiness. He has strangled himself and his family. What is the benefit of living like this, going through so much pain? This is not qurbani.' At that moment, Allah, to Jamaluddin's immense relief, seemed to intervene. As the muezzin in the mosque opposite started to call out 'Allahu Akbar, Allahu Akbar' Jamaluddin asked to be excused and I left them to their prayers.

After that day, every time I went to Old Delhi I feared I would find the kheer shop closed. Then one day I arrived to find a different kind of change. The partition was gone, the shop was sporting new tables, shiny aluminium chairs and there was a new sign proclaiming 'Old Kheer Shop'. Jamaluddin laughed at my shock. 'We solved all our problems. I waited for Allah and our problems got solved. All that stuff I told you, it's all fine now.' The twinkle in his eyes was back and none of the family ever said another word on the matter.

Despite the family harmony and flashy new furniture, I don't expect the kheer wallahs to expand into the food courts of South Delhi malls, although as Madhubala and Ochterlony's begum found, stranger things have happened to Old Delhi wallahs. For four generations, the men of the Siddique family have risen every day at dawn to begin the long, slow process of making the day's batch of kheer and are mostly resigned to their kismet—the life Allah has chosen for them. I think the same might be said for the goat who enjoyed one more year of munching and grew so fat that by the end it occupied half the shop. As Jamaluddin always tells me as I sit nibbling his creamy kheer, 'I was born here, I live here, I will go from here.'

Korma, Kheer and Kismet

BADE MIAN'S KHEER

SERVES 4

Kheer is normally made with white sugar but I used jaggery to try and replicate Bade Mian's fudgy flavour and colour. I'm not sure if my kheer had 'the blessings of Allah' but it was very good.

INGREDIENTS

- 1 litre full cream milk
- 50 gms rice (I used broken Basmati)
- 3-4 tbsp jaggery
- Ground seeds of 2 green cardamom

METHOD

Wash the rice and soak in fresh water for about one hour, then drain. Bring the milk to a boil and add the rice and cardamom powder. Simmer over very low heat until the milk has thickened and the rice has almost completely disintegrated. Stir in jaggery to taste and leave on the heat until dissolved. Serve warm or cold.

TEN

Mughal Breakfasts and Jalebi Brunches

The temperature in Delhi had dropped by thirty degrees in the space of a few weeks. Sixteen million bodies had gone into shock, shivering and snuffling as the freezing Himalayan air surrounded us like a blast chiller. Suddenly it was warmer outside than inside our drafty cold-floored homes. The children in our neighbourhood sat in the park to do their homework and old people dragged sofas out on to the street and sat there all day, swaddled in shawls and bobble hats, warming their joints and charging up on the midday sun like solar panels. In the absence of central heating, we piled quilts on the beds, and tried to remember where, nine months earlier, we'd stashed thick pyjamas, thermals and hot water bottles. Rickshaw wallahs, in their winter uniform of matching mufflers and neon-coloured sparkly sleeveless sweaters, stamped their feet and nursed steaming cups of chai. The signature scent of the season was 'eau de mothball', as thick tweedy jerkins and handmade woollens were hauled out of hibernation.

With the change in weather came a change of appetite. At home, for a brief few weeks we enjoyed hearty soups and stews and in Old Delhi, the street food was at its most tempting. The American writer Robert P. Coffin wrote in 1949, 'Weather, mother of good poetry, is also the mother of good breakfasts.' And, during the winter, Old Delhi boasts the mother and father of all breakfasts, a rich slow-cooked, eye-wateringly spicy meat stew called nihari, a dish which is thought to have originated in Shah Jahan's kitchens, designed as a way of clearing blocked royal sinuses. Its name comes from the Arabic word 'nahar' meaning morning, because it was traditionally prepared overnight and eaten first thing—during Ramzan it is sometimes eaten at sehri before the day's fast begins. It is a slow-cooked meal of fire, fat and unctuous buffalo or goat meat, often with a side order of brains, bone marrow or trotters, all mopped up with fluffy naan. It's definitely not for those who prefer to start the day with a bowl of muesli and low fat yogurt.

Nihari was one of the meals that kept the Mughal armies on their feet. But for your average, latter-day glutton, with no marching duties scheduled, the main challenge is to get out of bed at 5 a.m. on a freezing winter morning. A few winters passed before I finally managed it even persuading a friend, Tennille, a hardened Antipodean food warrior, to accompany me. I knew she was the right woman for the job when, in the taxi on the way, she told me she'd just returned from a food-centric holiday to San Francisco and spoke about the impressive quantity of food she had consumed. When I asked how she had managed to pack in so much eating, I'm sure she said something along the lines of Homer Simpson's, 'Easy, I discovered a meal between breakfast and brunch.'

We were looking for a well-known nihari joint called Kallu Nihari, so asked the taxi driver to drop us by Delite Cinema on Asaf Ali Road. We quickly discovered that this is also the drop-off point for much of Old Delhi's raw meat trade. We kept walking briskly, navigating piles of carcasses, rickshaws piled with goats' feet and mangy dogs making off with bags of bones. But we couldn't find what we were looking for. In the end, we asked a man who was walking with his small son and he told us that Kallu was only open in the evening and offered to take us to another nihari shop. He parked his son on a rickshaw then walked with us a few hundred yards into a street called Suiwalan. He stopped at a little shop and told us to sit on the metal bench outside. This, he said, was Ghaffar's nihari—'better than Kallu'. He hurried off back to his son and we ordered two plates of nihari. One of the shop's workers brought us some tea from one of Old Delhi's eternal teapots—so strong, it tasted as though it had been bubbling away at least as long as the nihari. Old Delhi tea, I thought, is a bit like sourdough bread—a little of the previous day's tea is carried over as a starter for the next day; it was just possible that our brew that morning contained the essence of those from Mughal times.

While we waited, I watched the man at the stove and noted that he passed my street vendor demeanour test. I've discovered that the men who make the best dishes in Old Delhi exude a serene, calm confidence in the food they're serving and a meticulous attention to detail for even the simplest of dishes. It's there on the faces of the cooks at Aslam Chicken Corner in Matia Mahal, and the old man near the Paranthe Wali Gali who makes hundreds of perfect little nan khatai biscuits every day. You'll see it at Sharmaji's spice shop in Lal Kuan and even in the inscrutable features of many khomcha wallahs. It's a look that says, 'This is the best there is, take it or leave it.'

It was a look that was definitely on the face of Mohammed Shahid, grandson of the nihari shop's founder Abdul Ghaffar. His dish is made from exactly the right cut of beef, containing enough marbling of fat to produce a rich, rib-sticking sauce and cooked for so long that the flesh can be nudged softly from the bone with the fresh naan. The flavours of his nihari were not just well acquainted with each other, they'd had time to form a deep and lasting bond. Shahid was attentive, watching us while we ate, ready with extra bread, slivers of ginger and chilli, or a piece of meat if required but he was unsurprised at our sighs of delight. As we sat devouring the warming nihari, I think Tennille and I both decided it was probably the finest breakfast this side of the Mughal Empire and, possibly, a cure for whatever ails you.

After Ghaffar's nihari I ate nothing for the rest of the day, but most winter trips to Old Delhi weren't complete without a trip to the Old and Famous Jalebi Wala, a much loved street food landmark, where crowds frequently bring the intersection of Dariba Kalan and Chandni Chowk to a standstill. The first recorded mention of jalebis, from the Persian 'zoolbia', was in a 1450 description of a feast at which they were served. A Kannada document from 1600 describes the jalebi as 'looking like a creeper, tasty as nectar'. They may well be one of the most efficient and satisfying sugar hits—

hot crispy coils of deep-fried batter drenched in fragrant syrup. They are especially welcome in cold winter months when we can convince ourselves of the need for extra sugar and fat. Just watching the cook pipe the batter into the huge vat of bubbling ghee and seeing the jalebis progress from white to sunny orange is instantly cheering.

One winter day, when I'd satisfied my initial sugar craving and was waiting for the rest of my order to be packed to take home, I tried, as I always did, to persuade one of the shop's owners Abhishek Jain to tell me the secret of his family's marvellous jalebis. He usually replied with an inscrutable smile and told me that 'nobody outside of the family had ever been shown or told the recipe' but I had nevertheless gleaned a few facts. I knew that the jalebi batter is made from 75 per cent white flour and 25 per cent ground urad dal mixed into a thick paste. At the end of each day, a little of the batter is left in a brass pot to ferment slightly, then used as the base for the next day's batch. This process is known as 'khamir uthana' and it makes the batter ferment just enough to put some air and a slight tang in the jalebis. The brass pot also imparts a unique flavour to the batter. The real magic, the Jalebi Walas always told me, happens in the syrup—they claim it takes twenty-two hours to make—and on that subject I had never been able to make any progress. That winter day, though, my bag of hot jalebis came with a surprise invitation from Abhishek, 'Come to my house for brunch on Sunday and we'll tell you all about the jalebis.'

The Jains live in two spacious apartments in Civil Lines, an affluent residential neighbourhood of North Delhi originally built by the British Raj for its senior officers. Abhishek and his wife and daughter live in one, his parents, Kailash and Anita, in the other. Brunch was to be in his parents' home where we all got to know each other over cauliflower and pea samosas, little triangles of shahi tukda, creamy sandesh and, of course, a few jalebis. It didn't take long for conversation to drift back to Old Delhi, or the place Abhishek's mother still calls 'sheher', where the family lived until recently. It wasn't so long ago, she told me, that South Delhi, now the capital's most affluent area, was an uncivilized jungle. She remembered how alarmed her sister had been when she left Dariba Kalan in 1974 to live with her husband's family in South Delhi. 'She was scared; she saw only forest and pigs. At that time they (inhabitants of South Delhi) were living in villages. The Mughals had dotted monuments all over, so little pockets were there but Old Delhi was the main city...' Kailash, like his wife, barely out of his fifties, remembered trams and 'when the Yamuna came into Chandni Chowk'. When he was a child, he said, there was still a family living in the Bhagirath Palace, and they kept their horses on the ground floor. The building, which was originally built for one of the great characters of eighteenth-century Shahjahanabad,

Begum Samru, is now the site of an unruly wholesale market for light fittings, electrical and surgical equipment. 'In 1964, there was only one car in Dariba,' he said, shaking his head at present-day congestion. 'That was ours—an Ambassador.'

When the family moved out of Old Delhi a few years ago, they found they couldn't sleep in their new neighbourhood—it was too quiet. 'Life is there,' said Anita Jain, meaning Old Delhi, sheher. 'From the balcony you can see so much of drama, so much of life. All the khomcha wallahs, pani puri, chaat, lassi, so much of food… Here everything is very quiet. There's no stimulation here.' Her son Abhishek agreed. 'You see different characters [there]. People that you don't find in South Delhi, only in Chandni Chowk. Every morning I'll show you a hundred different characters.'

Mrs Anita Jain wanted to show me her wedding jewellery. As the matriarch of street food royalty I was expecting hers to be an impressive collection, but the box she opened contained a single traditional red and green kundan set—one modest enamel necklace with matching bracelet and earrings. It was, she said, the only piece of wedding jewellery she had left; everything else—a substantial and valuable collection, including a set of gold pistols that was given to her by her mother and mother-in-law when she married Kailash—was sold in 1980 to save the family business.

The Jalebi Wala story began almost a hundred years before that when Nem Chand Jain, Kailash's father, left his ancestral village near Agra with nothing to his name but a fifty-paise dowry from his seven-year-old wife. Determined to make his fortune in the city, for years Nem Chand was an itinerant hawker selling rabri until a Muslim trader, Shamsuddin Ifran, who owned a shop on the corner of Dariba Kalan and Chandni Chowk, allowed him to set up a permanent stall on the pavement outside. Eventually, Nem Chand's jalebis made him richer than his landlord, enabling him to build a large haveli for his family in nearby Gali Khazanchi. In the wave of violence between Hindus and Muslims before Partition, Nem Chand hid his benefactor in the haveli for ten days. When Shamsuddin Ifran was forced to flee to Pakistan, he gave his shop over to the man who had sat on the pavement outside his shop for over forty years. 'You saved my life, lalaji,' he said. 'You occupy this place.'

A few weeks after our brunch in Civil Lines, Kailash took me to visit the haveli where Shamsuddin Ifran had been hidden. Gali Khazanchi, off Dariba Kalan, is easy to walk straight past, one of a thousand similar lanes. But as with much of Old Delhi, it's rich with history. First he showed me the remains of another haveli, built for the men the gully is named after: Shah Jahan's accountants. Underneath, he said, there was still a tunnel leading to the Red Fort along which Mughal fortunes were once transported. Further down the street, the Jains' haveli was hidden from the main thoroughfare and we entered it through a grand, but almost obscured, intricately panelled wooden door. Inside, the haveli is a three storey, sixty-room property but one which has seen better days. Kailash pointed out the room where his son was born in 1979. 'Under our bed we had a pull-out bed for Abhishek to sleep on.' As Kailash began to build the business again, the family went to live above the shop in 1988. When Abhishek married, he rode a horse from the shop to the airy apartments in Civil Lines.

Now the Jains' haveli is only home to a couple of cousins prepared to put up with crumbling walls and leaky roofs but it is still just possible to imagine the splendour in which their ancestor Nem Chand lived, with its teak panelling and German mosaic floors. 'We were famous throughout Delhi,' said Kailash. 'The only shop where you could buy jalebis at that time.' In fact, Nem Chand Jain made so much money, he ran out of places to keep it. 'At that time, nobody used to keep money in the bank—nobody knew how to sign anything.' His solution was to fill up the empty ghee tins with the shop's takings. 'They were 15-kg tins of ghee. He used to convert the tins and put a lock on them then fill them with paper money. There must have been fifty to sixty containers. At today's rates, it would be crores [millions].' Keeping that amount of money was perhaps part of the reason the family kept so many weapons. Kailash estimated they had around two hundred guns but Nem Chand also devised his own novel form of security. He told everyone that whenever he left the room where the money was kept, two snakes appeared to guard it. No one ever saw the snakes, but no one ever went near Nem Chand's ghee tins.

Over several brunches that winter, the Jain family told me more about the family history. Nem Chand's first son, Gyan Chand, who was born in 1921, started working in the shop when he was barely in his teens and built up a formidable, gun-toting reputation for himself. They showed me old family pictures of him—a burly young man in an immaculate white coat dripping with diamonds and gold and a round of bullets draped across his shoulder. 'He was quite a character,' said Abhishek. 'When he was sitting in the shop, he used to always carry a revolver. His son was arrested once and Gyan Chand went to the police station and said, "You let him go or I'll kill all of you." They let [the son] go. Yes, he was quite a character.' He too amassed a fortune. 'Every day he used to buy a gold coin for his wife,' said Abhishek. 'Just imagine how many gold coins she must be having.' Quick as a flash, his father did a quick calculation, 'A gold coin a day for twenty to twenty-five years? More than 9,000 gold coins.'

Gyan Chand's brother, Kailash, was born in 1952 and by 1970 he too was working in the shop. Their father, Nem Chand, continued to come to the shop every day right up to his death at ninety-seven. After his death, the two brothers worked together until Gyan Chand's death in 1980. The shop's legal status then took two years to settle in the High Court as Gyan Chand's sons challenged Kailash for ownership. In the end, a closed auction was held between family members and a recently married Anita secured the winning bid by selling her jewellery and gold guns. The five and a half lakh rupees she raised were enough to pay off all of her husband's nephews and ensure no future dispute. I wondered how she had managed to hold on to the kundan set. 'That type of jewellery doesn't keep its value, otherwise [it] would have been sold as well.'

So in 1982, with nothing but his father's recipe and an empty shop, Kailash set about re-building the business from scratch. 'When my father started again,' says Abhishek, 'they had nothing. They lived above the shop.' What he lacked in cash, Kailash made up for in charisma and soon the shop was the talk of the town again. Cricketers, politicians and Bollywood stars like Imtiaz Ali and Akshay Kumar soon beat a path to Chandni Chowk for their jalebis. 'Raj and Randhir Kapoor used to come in the early hours to avoid the crowds.' The shop, he said, never closes and he never switches off, even when he's physically away from it. 'My mind is always over there.'

When his turn came, Abhishek didn't think twice about following in his father's footsteps, or what the kheer-making Siddique family would call his kismet. Despite being educated at one of South Delhi's most prestigious private schools and his father urging him to consider doing an MBA or studying abroad, he told me he only ever wanted to work in the shop and was happy to sit for long hours every day at one of Old Delhi's busiest corners. 'It's been here for so many years, why give it to someone else and [risk] them spoiling it?'

I asked how he planned to make his mark on the business. Will he expand? Franchise? Open branches in South Delhi's many new malls? Father and son were both adamant this wouldn't happen. The family has a rule that their jalebis should not be made anywhere but Dariba Kalan, although Kailash said they did once make an exception when Prime Minister Atal Behari Vajpayee asked them to come and make jalebis at his home. Generally, though, they believe expansion and diversification means having to trust people outside the family, which would affect quality and profit. Kailash described how outsiders could easily ruin the business. 'Every week I have offers to open shops all over. But this thing has to be done by the self of our family members only. You give someone [else] 5 kg ghee for the pan, they put on the gas and burn it—no sale is there.' No one, he said, would ensure quality is maintained like a family member, and the family's reputation would be destroyed. It would be very easy for dishonest staff to cheat them. Abhishek gave an example—'Diwali was very busy for us. The very next day after Diwali, I went to the shop—I was in the shop till 11 at night and nobody came to buy anything. Then, at that moment, a guy came in and ordered 26 kg of jalebis. With dishonest staff I would never have got to know about that late order.' Crucially, to diversify would also mean sharing the secret family recipe. 'How can you let the recipe out for everyone to know? Then everyone can make our jalebis. That is why we can't do franchising.' Kailash took out a note from his pocket and summed up his (and most other Old Delhi wallahs') business management philosophy. 'Listen, this is a five-hundred-rupee note. If it is in my pocket it is mine. If it is in your pocket it is yours. If it ends up in someone else's pocket I can never know because it's a cash business. There is no way of trust.'

Over the years of visiting the Old and Famous Jalebi Wala, I had managed to piece together how the jalebi batter is made. I had always been told the magic was in the sugar syrup and that its formula could never be divulged. To everyone's surprise that day, perhaps mine most of all, Kailash suddenly said, 'The key to the jalebis is the syrup, and the key to the syrup is cleaning the sugar.' He paused, as if trying to decide whether or not to continue. 'When you boil the sugar, there's a lot of dirt which comes out of it. We call it "cutting the dirt" in Hindi. Before adding the spices, you have to clean that sugar.' Abhishek looked shocked, then laughed, 'I told you a long time back, the thing is in the syrup, not in the jalebis. I could not tell you but right now he is telling you how it is made—when you boil a huge quantity of sugar, we add water to it and the dirt comes out.' 'That's it?' I asked. 'That's the secret that's passed down from father to son?' 'That's it,' Kailash replied. 'That's what gets passed down from father to son.' I was lost for words but somehow managed to strike while the iron was hot. 'I don't suppose I could come and watch you make the syrup?' Four faces bore the same expression—don't push your luck!

JALEBIS

MAKES AT LEAST 24

The Old and Famous Jalebi Walas never let me in on their secret recipe but I did glean a few details over the years, like the use of urad dal in the batter and overnight fermenting. This lemon-flavoured syrup is completely unorthodox, but tastes very good.

INGREDIENTS
  Batter
  110 gms plain flour (maida)

40 gms urad dal, ground to a powder

125 gms yogurt

150 ml water

Ghee for frying

Syrup

250 gms sugar

500 ml water

3 cardamom pods

1 strip lemon zest

METHOD

In a large bowl, whisk together the flour, ground urad dal, yogurt and water until you have a smooth batter. Cover the bowl and leave it in a warm place for at least 24 hours.

To make the syrup, put all the ingredients in a pan and boil until the liquid has thickened.

To fry the jalebis, heat 4 cm depth of ghee in a kadhai over medium heat. Whisk the batter once more and spoon it into a piping bag. Squeeze neat spirals into the hot ghee, turning the jalebis over a few times until they are golden brown. If they brown too quickly, lower the heat slightly.

With a slotted spoon, remove the jalebis, drain excess ghee at the side of the pan and transfer straight into the syrup. Let the jalebis soak up some of the syrup before serving.

ELEVEN

God's Own Street Food

By January the sky was, at best, a soft grey marl but some days there was just a gradual shift from ebony to slate. Planes at Indira Gandhi International Airport were grounded by fog, lungs were attacked by a thick yellowish pall of smog and, as temperatures hovered near zero, many of the city's homeless people died on its freezing cold pavements.

But for food lovers, those very cold weeks in Old Delhi had some compensations. The markets were full of vibrant fruit and vegetables—spinach, mustard leaf, peas, beans and deep red 'desi' carrots; strawberries, citrus fruits and the brilliant bunched orange orbs of ras bhari (cape gooseberries) beaming at us. Winter also brought the new season's jaggery, and pushcarts groaned under tons of the freshly made rocky lumps of crystallized sugar-cane juice. At Ashok and Ashok I discovered that jaggery was served with their mutton korma during the winter months because it '[helped] the ghee go down' and wondered whether it might be time to check both my cholesterol and sugar levels. The arrival of the jaggery also meant that the chikki makers were out in force and, in a tiny lane off Gali Batashan, I discovered a whole row of shops selling nothing but the sticky discs studded with sesame, cashews, peanuts, even rose petals.

One of the great highlights of the winter is a heavenly milky dessert that makes a brief but unforgettable earthly appearance in the gullies of Old Delhi almost as soon as the last Diwali firecracker has fizzled. From then until Holi, the daulat ki chaat vendors wander through the bazaars, their snowy platters dazzling in the pale sunshine, as if a dozen small, perfectly formed clouds have dropped from the sky.

Daulat ki chaat (meaning 'snack of wealth') is probably Old Delhi's most surprising street food. Anyone expecting the punchy, spicy flavours usually suggested by the word 'chaat' will be disappointed. It resembles uncooked meringue and the taste is shocking in its subtlety, more molecular gastronomy than raunchy street food, a light foam that disappears instantly on the tongue, leaving behind the merest hint of sweetness, cream, saffron, sugar and nuts; tantalizing, almost not there. I've often wondered if daulat ki chaat is a preview of what might be on the menu should we make it as far as the pearly gates.

The means by which a pail of milk is transformed into the food of the gods, though, is the stuff of Old Delhi legend rather than of the food lab. First, so the story goes, milk and cream have to be whisked by hand before dawn (preferably under the light of a full moon) into a delicate froth, then left out on grass to set by the 'tears of shabnam' (morning dew)—but not too many, nor too few. At daybreak, the surface of the froth is touched with saffron and silver leaf and served with nuts and bura (unrefined sugar). Daulat ki chaat is only made in the coolest months because at the first ray of sunshine, it starts to collapse. It doesn't travel well either—to enjoy this very local speciality, a winter pilgrimage to the shady gullies of Old Delhi has to be made.

As with most legends, this one was proving impossible to verify. The origins of the dish are unclear but it has all the hallmarks of Mughal culinary splendour. Food writer Madhur Jaffrey remembers it as a breakfast treat from her childhood in Delhi in the 1930s and wrote about it in the 1970s:

Early in the morning an old lady in an immaculate ankle-length skirt and a well-starched white muslin bodice and head covering appeared at our gate. On her head she carried an enormous brass tray, and on the tray were mutkainas, partially baked red clay cups containing the frothy ambrosia. The recipe was—and always has been—a mystery. I remember cornering the lady in white at about age 11 and begging her to tell me how she made it, but she shook her head, saying, "Oh, child, I am the only woman left in the whole city of Delhi who can make this. I am so old and it is such hard work that I only go to all the trouble because your grandmother and I have known each other for so many years. How do I make it? It needs all the right conditions. First I take milk and add dried sea foam to it. Then I pour the mixture into clay cups. I have to climb up to the roof and leave the cups there overnight in the chill air. Now the most important ingredient is the dew. If there is no dew, the froth will not form. If there is too much dew, that is also bad. The dew you have to leave to the gods. In the early morning, if the froth is good, I sprinkle the cups with khurchan [milk that has been boiled until all the liquid has evaporated and the sweetened solids have peeled off in thin layers]. Then I sprinkle pistachio nuts over that."

The lady in white is gone now, as is her recipe, but the taste of that cold daulat-ki-chat *lingers still*. [*]

The lady in white can rest in peace and Jaffrey herself might be surprised to know that there has been something of a Renaissance in the supply of angel food to the masses. As amazed bloggers and food writers have begun to rediscover the dish, there has been a renewed interest in this culinary treasure. Five years ago there were only a couple of daulat ki chaat carts in Old Delhi; now there are perhaps fifteen to twenty. Jaffrey should probably be more concerned about the fate of khurchan—there is just one shop left, Hazari Lal Jain Khurchan Wale, that sells these silky white 'scrapings', down at the Dariba Kalan end of Kinari Bazaar. If you visit early in the morning, before the wedding shoppers descend, you'll see Hazari Lal's men out on the street painstakingly reducing and scraping milk in giant cauldrons.

The preparation of daulat ki chaat is much more secretive. Like Jaffrey, for many daulat ki chaat seasons I had begged the vendors to tell me about their dish; every winter I tried, and failed, to persuade them to let me watch it being made. I had found an occasional mention of the dish in cookbooks, but with no historical context

---

[*] *Gourmet Magazine*, 1974

or explanation. I had never met anyone, even the most enthusiastic of cooks, who made it at home—perhaps the 'tears of dew' and 'sea foam' are just too difficult to source. I decided I couldn't let another winter pass without uncovering the mysteries of daulat ki chaat. I started pestering anyone I could think of to introduce me to daulat ki chaat wallahs and persuade one of them to show me the sweet being made. As in previous years, I made very little headway. There was, however, universal consensus on two things—that daulat ki chaat was now made in an unromantic machine in some grubby godown; and that no one would ever show me the process because they were adding God knows what to make it set. I ran into my guruji Rahul Verma at the Foreign Correspondents' Club one night and he wasn't encouraging. 'They'll never show you how it's made,' he declared definitively. 'They're almost certainly adding something to the milk to make it set and also they wouldn't want you to see the conditions in which they're operating.'

Then, during one of the Civil Lines brunches, 'Jalebi Wala' Abhishek Jain said he would be happy to help. I jumped at the offer even though it was issued with dire warnings. 'If you see that place where they make it you'll never eat it again,' he said. 'I don't think you'll be able to survive that place, it's very dirty.' But there were just a few weeks left of the daulat ki chaat season and the prospect of its mysteries remaining unsolved for another year was unbearable. The next day, Abhishek sent me a telephone number of a daulat ki chaat vendor, but when I called and spoke in my basic Hindi I was too easily fobbed off. Christmas came and went and we were plunged into the coldest days of the year and I knew my daulat ki chaat days were numbered. Throughout January, text messages were exchanged back and forth between Abhishek and I, mine increasingly desperate as the season neared its end.

By early February, when there were a few alarmingly warm and spring-like days, Abhishek must have felt under siege as I stepped up the pressure. Finally, he told me that he had asked the local police to get involved and promised to set up a meeting within a week. I didn't want to get anyone into trouble, I said. 'Madam, these people only get to be there because the cops allow them— hawking is not allowed. So I've already told one cop to find me the thing, where it is made.' A few more days passed and Abhishek told me that one daulat ki chaat vendor, Rakesh Kumar, was willing to show me his chaat being made but was demanding 5,000 rupees in exchange. Holi colours were already appearing in the markets, a sure sign of the imminent summer heat, and of the disappearance of daulat ki chaat makers, so in desperation, I quickly agreed. A final SMS instruction arrived—'Rakesh Kumar, 84 Ghanta, Sita Ram Bazaar, reach here by 4.30am tmrw mrng. Pay as u feel like. Don't worry he will help u.' I felt a rush of relief and excited anticipation that this could be the moment I would finally get to watch an Old Delhi dish being made.

At 3.30 a.m. the next morning, Mr Mishra, our security guard, was curled up on the porch and I had to climb over him to get to the waiting taxi. One of our local taxi drivers, an old Sikh man named Mr Singh, had arrived to pick me up, probably assuming it was an airport or station run. When I said I was going into Old Delhi he looked perplexed and for a moment I thought he was going to refuse to take me. He started up the old Ambassador car, still looking as if he hoped I'd change my mind en route. We glided through the leafy deserted streets of Lutyens Delhi, the boulevards of power where the nation-shapers were all tucked up for the night.

Within fifteen minutes we had reached the Sri Digambar Jain Lal Mandir guarding the entrance to Chandni Chowk and although the daytime chaos of cars, rickshaws and carts was missing, I could see there was still plenty of activity on the dark streets. Sikhs were milling around the Gurudwara Sis Ganj Sahib and the streets were lined with haulage trucks being loaded with everything from saris, shoes and paper to grain, spices and kitchen equipment, at the start of long journeys all over India. A still-baffled Mr Singh announced that we'd arrived in Chandni Chowk in a tone suggesting that for the life of him he couldn't work out why I would want to be here. I told him we needed to go a bit further and directed him to the end of Chandni Chowk and on through Katra Bariyan and Lal Kuan. Hauz Qazi Chowk resembled a military checkpoint and we had stop for me to tell police officers what I was doing. When I told them I had come to watch daulat ki chaat being made, they looked just as baffled as Mr Singh but eventually allowed us to proceed into Sitaram Bazaar.

Following Abhishek's instructions, towards the end of Sitaram Bazaar we stopped at a police box. A group of officers came over to the taxi and confirmed we were in the right place. But which of the many dingy doorways and alleys could lead to the daulat ki chaat headquarters? I dialled the number Abhishek had given me for Rakesh Kumar, expecting it to be switched off, but it was answered immediately by a man who said he was coming to fetch me. Seconds later, a nervous young man came scurrying out of an alleyway and I instantly recognized him from the daulat ki chaat stalls in Dariba Kalan. He quickly confirmed he was Babu Ram Kumar, younger brother of Rakesh, and as I followed him back into the gully I sensed the men in uniform behind me twiddling moustaches and scratching their heads.

The gully was a filthy dead end strewn with garbage and rubble, pitch dark and silent apart from a distant rhythmic sound. As we walked through a once-grand archway and into a small room, the sound grew louder and I was suddenly enveloped in the pungent smells of milk, last night's dinner and life being lived in a confined space. Inside, most of the room was taken up by a bed and a mattress on the floor, both packed with people sleeping. I couldn't see any faces but in one corner a long pigtail peeked out, in another there was the sound of a child coughing, a bare leg here, an arm there. Strung between two corners there was a rope weighed down by the family's shabby clothing: three pieces of a woman's faded yellow salwar kameez set, woollen baby clothes and well-worn men's work trousers. A single bare light bulb hung from a crumbling ceiling beam and bathed everything in grey. Dangling from hooks on the peeling walls, which may once have been blue, there were brooms, plastic carrier bags stuffed with dried-leaf plates, a giant grater with khoya stuck in its teeth, cooking pots and a lopsided clock. The floor was partially covered with old rice sacks and under the bed was a tub full of stainless steel plates and a basket containing leftover rotis. Next to it was a small stove, a blackened chai pan and a plastic tub of what I recognized as the khoya and sugar toppings for daulat ki chaat. All of the food was uncovered, an open invitation, I registered fleetingly, to any self-respecting rodent.

Then I noticed the milk pails and three large platters of gleaming white froth and suddenly I saw where the rhythmic sound was coming from. A young man with tousled hair and dressed in clothes he had obviously slept in was perched on a low stool tucked behind the door, tugging on two ropes as if trying to control a particularly unruly stallion. The ropes were attached to a giant churning stick in a large aluminium pot from which was emerging something that looked exactly like sea foam. The pot was set over an even larger basin filled with ice.

As the sleepers turned and stirred, moustaches, legs, ponytails moved. Then one of the men flung off his covers and threw out his legs. The zipper of his trousers was undone, revealing muddy brown-coloured underpants. Still sleeping soundly, his hand moved automatically towards the opening. Quickly, and probably hoping I hadn't noticed, Babu Ram turned and gave the man a kick before throwing the cover back over him.

'Chai?' asked Babu Ram, perhaps to distract me, and quickly busied himself at the stove. While he stirred the pan, he told me that his family had been making daulat ki chaat in Delhi for about a hundred years and that they make it the same way today as they always have. Every evening, thirty-five kilos of milk and fifteen kilos of cream are delivered from a dairy. The three brothers of the family get up at 3 a.m. and froth the milk until nine. He broke off now and then to dismantle the strings from the churning stick and scrape off the foam that had gathered and to lay it gently in a wide, shallow metal dish. From the already full platters, he drained off the milk that had gathered in the bottom back into the whisking tub. When he and his brother have whisked all the milk, he told me, they sleep for a couple of hours then go out into Old Delhi to sell the daulat ki chaat. The brothers work every day between Diwali and Holi, then return to their village in Uttar Pradesh to look after the family farm.

Demand for daulat ki chaat has grown in recent years, he said, and the Kumars now have five pitches including one at the busy Paranthe Wali Gali and two in Dariba Kalan, not far from the Old and Famous Jalebi Walas. When I asked if they were ever tempted to speed up the process by using electric mixers, he shook his head.

Electric mixers, he said, just don't give the same results as hand churning.

I sat and watched the brothers at work for some time, lulled by the gentle sounds of the wordless, repetitive churning and scraping. My soporific state was interrupted when I got up to leave and Babu Ram reminded me about the payment. I handed over the 5,000 rupees and made my way back down the dark alley, relieved to find Mr Singh waiting at the end of it.

Later that day, after I'd taken a nap and my early morning adventure started to seem like a dream, I thought about Abhishek's warnings and wondered if my visit to the Kumars' dirty and disorganized workshop had taken away a little of the magic and mystery of daulat ki chaat or even put me off eating it forever. I'd certainly discovered that morning dew and moonlight aren't strictly necessary and if there is any magic involved it is administered by poor farmers from UP with tousled hair and threadbare clothes rather than by angels. But I was reassured that daulat ki chaat is still made in the traditional way, relying on cold nights, simple ingredients and hours of whisking by hand. And I know that every year there will always be a moment just after Diwali when there will be no more welcome sight than the daulat ki chaat wallahs' snowy platters lighting up Old Delhi's wintry lanes.

DAULAT KI CHAAT

SERVES 4-6

Most of the recipes in this book demonstrate how very humble ingredients can be transformed into dishes of great beauty, flavour and depth. Here, milk is transformed into something halfway between a soufflé and a cloud, worthy of any five-star restaurant, anywhere in the world. But that transformation is hard, hard work as I found out on that winter morning when I visited the Kumar family's daulat ki chaat workshop. In line with tradition, when it came to trying to recreate the dish in my own kitchen, I started before first light although, sadly, there was no full moon. For about one hour I tried to whisk the milk with a wooden churning stick, a small version of the one I watched the Kumar brothers using, but I only succeeded in producing a few bubbles which collapsed immediately whenever I paused. Eventually, I switched to an electric hand-held mixer and the bubbles gradually turned into something a little more solid. Even when using modern kitchen appliances like a fridge and an electric mixer, the daulat ki chaat was an arduous dish to produce, making me marvel all the more at the Old Delhi version which relies solely on cold nights and muscle power.

INGREDIENTS

- 1 litre full cream milk
- 400 ml cream (malai)
- A few ground strands of saffron mixed with a little milk
- Caster sugar
- Pistachio nuts, chopped
- Silver leaf (varq)

METHOD

In a large bowl, mix together the milk and cream and leave overnight in the fridge. In the (very early) morning, whisk the milk and cream until a thick froth forms on the surface—I averaged about one tablespoon every five minutes. With a slotted spoon, carefully place this froth on a wide platter and leave somewhere cold to set—I left mine on a window ledge in the cold morning air. Continue until all the milk has been whisked, pouring off any milk that gathers in the bottom of the platter.

Sprinkle a few drops of the saffron liquid on the surface of the daulat ki chaat along with some silver leaf and chopped pistachio nuts. Sprinkle with caster sugar when serving.

TWELVE

At Home in Old Delhi

In Scotland I always fear the onset of spring as the start of a prolonged period of dashed hopes when, for every longed-for sign of warmer weather—swallows returning from their winter migration and hedgerows budding—there is usually a week of rain or snow. In Delhi, 'spring' is the term used to describe the handful of perfect days between discarding hot water bottles and phoning the air-conditioning engineers. It's a brief meteorological sweet spot when we all rush to spend as much time as possible outdoors in the sunshine and the parks fill again with families picnicking as if the end of the world were nigh. Because we know that all too soon, for brutal, searing months on end, it will be too hot to linger outside and our only consolation will be mangoes. Unfortunately, spring is also the time when the mysterious 'change of season' maladies sweep the capital; bodies which have ricocheted between temperatures of almost zero in January and sudden intense warmth go into shock. Instead of enjoying the glorious weather, many of us are sick and miserable. I'd always been sceptical about this seasonal syndrome, but this year it was my turn and I was laid low with fever.

When I started to feel a bit better, Dean, eager not to let the good weather pass without a jaunt to his favourite restaurant, suggested lunch at Ashok and Ashok. It seemed like a good idea but once we got there I was feeling too weak and queasy to eat, so I slumped on a nearby ledge to watch the comings and goings around the shop. As they bustled around getting ready for the lunchtime trade, the staff took pity on me and brought me a bottle of Sprite and, for the first time, answered some of my questions. I spoke to the man who is always front of house at the shop—his eagle eyes everywhere, keeping staff in line, watching for plates that need to be refilled, making sure the rotis keep flowing. He's always immaculately shaved, with jet black oiled hair, neatly pressed clothes and clerical glasses. He is also usually the man with the hand on the cash box, which I assumed meant he was a close family member. His name is Kamal Puri, he told me; his sister Pinky is Ashok Bhatia's widow. I asked him if he could tell me a little about Ashok Bhatia. He shrugged as if to say there wasn't much to tell. Bhatia owned a dairy in Laxmi Nagar in East Delhi, but lived in Sadar Bazaar where he was friends with Ashok Arora with whom he'd opened the restaurant. I asked if Puri had heard all the rumours about the founders. 'Yes,' he said, 'but Ashok Bhatia was not a gangster, he was a nice, innocent person.' What about his partner? 'Arora was not a gangster. But if you do something he doesn't like, he beat you.' Once the two Ashoks opened the shop, though, according to Puri, Arora seemed to undergo something of a transformation. 'When he started business, he changed his nature, totally changed, kind to everyone.' Where did Puri think the rumours came from? He said he didn't know but thought it might have something to do with Ashok Arora's younger brother. In fact, the brother, he said, was as far as he knew, still in jail. In any case, it seemed the Bhatias were resigned to their shop's reputation.

'Some stories you cannot change,' he said. 'People can say whatever they like.'

By then, the shop was getting busy and Puri said he would have to get back to work. I quickly asked him, 'Where do you make the korma? Would I be able to watch?' He laughed. 'That is a secret, only Bhatia's son Monny and the cook know the recipe.' He left me to get on with the business of serving one of Old Delhi's best plates of food and I settled back on my ledge, wishing I felt well enough to eat. As the hungry crowds ate and the pots of korma started to empty, the waiters started shouting, 'Mistry! Mistry!' I looked around and watched one of them run to a building on the other side of the street. On the roof of the building a man was leaning over the side and lowering a large bucket, attached to a rope, down to the pavement below. The waiter who had crossed the street took out a heavy pot from the bucket and sent the empty one back up to the roof. I laughed and Puri caught my eye. 'So that's the kitchen?' I asked. 'Yes,' he said and went back to work. Once Dean had finished eating, we crossed the street to see if we could find the entrance to the rooftop kitchen. Eventually, we found it in a back lane and I started to walk towards the doorway. The secret of Ashok and Ashok's mutton korma was at the top of the stairs; all I had to do was take a few steps and I would see it being made. I don't know whether the 'change of season' had weakened not only my immune system but also my resolve to get to the bottom of the Ashok and Ashok mystery, but suddenly it just didn't feel important anymore. I turned around and walked back out. It wasn't until a few weeks later, when Ashok Arora's family, Kamlesh and Amit, invited me to celebrate Ashtami that I understood why.

To get to the Aroras' longed-for new home, I had to drive over to the other side of the Yamuna river, through miles of unruly urban sprawl where rickshaws and bullock carts fought for space

among thundering SUVs. On either side of the highway were all the signs of India's emerging middle class—hundreds of small private educational institutes offering courses in English, hotel management and engineering; property agents, gyms, branches of McDonalds, Benetton and Levi's. Beyond the main roads, as far as the eye could see, there were anonymous modern concrete suburbs, warrens of sweatshops and giant mountains of garbage and e-waste where children scavenged and played cricket. So I was pleasantly surprised to find the Aroras in one of Delhi's oldest areas, Shahdara, often referred to as 'Purani Dilli'. Their new apartment was in a small, quiet lane of brightly painted buildings in a brand new block that wasn't quite finished. Inside, their apartment was all sunny rooms and marble floors and Kamlesh was already hard at work in her neat, fitted kitchen. Amit was standing on the balcony surveying his new neighbourhood, looking anxious. For Ashtami, you need goddesses, he explained. Ashtami is part of the Navratri, a twice-yearly period of fasting that signals either the start of winter or the beginning of summer. Each day of the 'nine nights' involves a different set of rituals; on the eighth, people break their fast and invite nine little girls into their homes to represent the different forms of Durga. In Sadar Bazaar, there had been no shortage of 'goddesses'. 'In Sadar, there were only three Hindu families. Here in Shahdara everyone celebrates Ashtami and every little girl in the area is needed for the celebration.' Eventually, he decided to go outside and broaden his search.

While Amit rounded up the devis, I went to the kitchen where Kamlesh had kindly left the day's food preparation until the last moment so that I could watch her making it. The menu for Ashtami, she said, is always the same—chana puri and halwa. She said that although it is simple food, it is thought to keep people strong and ward off seasonal sniffles. As I still hadn't completely recovered from my 'change of season' woes, I couldn't wait to get started. First we made the sooji halwa and the kitchen filled with the sweet smell of bubbling semolina, sugar and ghee. Then Kamlesh finished off her chickpeas with rock salt and spices and heated a large pot of ghee for the puris. She let me take a turn at frying and puffing the breads but quickly decided I was too heavy-handed—'Halka! Halka!'—and took over before I could ruin the Ashtami feast. When she was satisfied with the food, she filled small bowls with chickpeas and halwa and laid them with a pile of puris in front of the family's shrine, alongside garlanded portraits of her husband Ashok and his father Bholanath Arora.

Soon a few tiny 'goddesses' in frothy chiffon dresses started to trickle in to the house, but for a while they were outnumbered by 'gods'. Eventually, Amit managed to shoo away the boys and organize the right ratio—nine girls and one boy—and Kamlesh began the puja. She lit a small dried piece of cow dung and the room filled with choking fumes. She knelt in front of the shrine and began the lengthy process of praying to the Goddess Durga.

The little girls sat cross-legged and silent, impeccably behaved throughout the puja, while Amit placed tilaks on their foreheads and tied sacred red threads on their tiny wrists. But once the formal parts of the puja had been completed, they started to grow restless as they sensed the reward for their patience was imminent. First we served them each a plate of warm chana puri and halwa, which they gobbled in seconds. Then they lined up in front of Amit and he piled their now empty plates with packets of crisps and chocolate. Before they left, he gave them each a twenty-rupee note and they clattered back down the stairs in a blur of shimmering pink, yellow, green and purple chiffon, like miniature ballroom dancers, off for the next lucrative round of devi duty.

As I drove back home, I realized that for the first time I had not asked Amit or his mother anything about Ashok and Ashok, even though more than a year had passed since the start of my feverish culinary quest and my file marked 'Authentic Old Delhi Street Food Recipes' was still almost empty. Five seasons had clicked over since that blisteringly hot afternoon with the Goggia family when I still believed that if I paid enough attention to the condition of a butcher's chopping block or the exact proportions of spices, I would uncover the mystery of Old Delhi's street food. And yet I certainly didn't feel the year had been wasted. After all, I understood quite early on that no amount of observation, persistence, and in some cases, bribery, would persuade street food vendors to part with their recipes. But the moment I realized that I was happy to simply eat rather than forensically examine their dishes came a little later. There was no epiphany, just a gradual realization that the magic of a great street food dish is not in any secret ingredient but in the formidable 'haath ki baat' of the generations of men who have made it. Jamaluddin may have said 'it's all from the blessings of Allah', but I think the master kheer wallahs and the many other great cooks in Old Delhi had, to paraphrase Malcolm Gladwell, reached greatness in their field at least partly by doing the same thing 10,000 times. I could never hope to recreate their dishes simply by watching them make it once. And even if I had the exact recipes for all the food I had eaten, there would always be one crucial ingredient missing—the actual experience of eating it on the street.

My year of enjoying and asking about Old Delhi street food hadn't led to a definitive record of how the dishes are made but it had given me something much more valuable. I had been invited into homes all over Old Delhi and beyond, treated like a long lost cousin and fed until I begged for mercy. When I think of that day I spent with the Goggias, it is the sharing of a family meal rather than the recipe I scribbled down which I will treasure forever. And during the many hours I spent in the Pimplapures' kitchen making Diwali treats, I felt like a new daughter-in-law being entrusted with the family's culinary legacy. I still have a weakness for jalebis but I prize more the memory of the long Sunday brunches with their 'Old and Famous' makers. Kamlesh Arora's Ashtami chana puri and halwa were uniquely precious, and not just because they finally saw off my 'change of season' ailments, but because I was being given the recipes for food she'd always cooked for her husband and son. The only time I ever saw a street food dish being made was in the small hours of a winter morning in Sitaram Bazaar, watching the Kumar bothers making daulat ki chaat. But what I'll remember more than the endless, backbreaking work of churning the milk is the steam rising from the cups of tea we sipped as the rest of the family slept around us.

As I drove home from Shahdara I looked back through the haze on the bridge and the road behind me suddenly seemed clear. The Old Delhi recipes I'd chased and sometimes caught weren't trophies after all. They were and always would be reminders of a time of warm welcomes and family feasts, and the moments when Goggia Uncle's mutton korma, Mr Naseem's sheer khurma and Kamlesh Arora's chana puri simply became the flavours of home.

KAMLESH ARORA'S CHANA PURI AND SOOJI HALWA

SERVES 10-12

INGREDIENTS

Chana

1 kg chickpeas

250 gms ghee

2 tsp red chilli powder

2½ tsp ground rock salt (sendha namak)

1 heaped tsp ground black pepper

METHOD

Boil the chickpeas until they are tender, then drain. In the same pan, melt the ghee and stir in the chilli powder, rock salt and pepper. Add the chickpeas and cook for a few moments until they are completely coated with the spiced ghee.

INGREDIENTS

Puri

150 gms wholemeal flour (atta)

½ tsp salt

125 ml water

250 gms ghee to fry the puris

METHOD

Mix together the flour, salt and water and knead for 5 minutes. Cover and rest the dough for at least 15 minutes.

When you're ready to serve the puris, heat the ghee in a kadhai. Put a little ghee on your hands and form the dough into small balls about the size of a walnut. Roll each ball out to about 1 mm thick. When the ghee is hot enough (when a small piece of dough immediately floats to the surface), slide in one puri at a time. Press down firmly on the puri with a metal slotted spoon and it should instantly puff up. Flip the puri over and press down again. When the puri is golden brown, flip it out on to some kitchen roll to drain off excess ghee.

INGREDIENTS

Sooji ka Halwa
250 gms ghee
250 gms semolina
250 gms sugar
1 litre water

METHOD

Melt the ghee in a large kadhai, then stir in the semolina. Cook over medium heat until the semolina has turned a rich golden brown and is giving off a toasted aroma. Stir in the sugar, then gradually add the water (be careful as it will splutter). Cook until almost all of the water has been absorbed but the mixture is still quite runny because it will thicken as it cools. Serve hot alongside the chana and puri.

Acknowledgements

I will never forget the extraordinary kindness that many have shown over the course of writing this book.

First, I was enormously fortunate to meet Hemanshu Kumar and his intrepid band of street food enthusiasts—Sachin Kalbag, Prajakta Samant, Supratim Sengupta, Nishant Jha—you opened my eyes to a whole new (to me) world of food and became treasured friends in the process.

Many have walked with me in Old Delhi and each enriched it in his or her own way. My 'guruji' Rahul Verma, with whom I have to race to keep up, has always been unstintingly generous with his compendious street food knowledge. Tennille Duffy, who loves Hemchand Ladli Prashad's milk cake as much as I do. Lucy Peck, Gaynor Barton and Surekha Narain all pointed out much that I would have missed.

Lucy also sent me a copy of her wonderfully definitive Old Delhi map, which, as well as being a work of great beauty, helped me reach some of the area's more obscure corners without mishap. Rahul Pal, my rickshaw driver, helped me interpret the map on the ground.

Sangita Singh and Siddhartha Singh helped me to a greater understanding of kheer wallah Jamaluddin's metaphors. Surya Bhattacharya and Sean McLain gave me a crash course in Durga Puja and Bengali food. Sarah Pearcey was an eagle-eyed early reader and chef Cameron Stauch helped enormously with recipe testing. Nilanjana Roy provided lunch and encouragement when they were most needed.

I'll be eternally grateful to the Pimplapure family for the wonderful times I've spent in their Sagar home and particularly to Nita, Meena and Asha and their cooks Ram Naresh and Suman who spent many hours sharing their recipes with me.

Thank you to all at Aleph for their patience and professionalism. In particular, I'll forever be in David Davidar's debt for his initial enthusiasm and then for giving me a deadline. Thank you to David Godwin and Anna Watkins in London for the hand-holding.

Of course, there would have been nothing to write about without the generosity and culinary skill of the people of Old Delhi. Thank you to everyone at Ashok and Ashok in Sadar Bazaar for making one of the world's best lunches and setting the year's quest in motion. I'll always treasure the afternoon spent at the Sadar Bazaar home of the Goggia family, the first of many to take me in and feed me. Enormous thanks to Amit and Kamlesh Arora, who may not have solved the Mutton Korma Mysteries for me but provided endless hospitality, kindness and games of pool for my husband and sons. Thank you to Mr Zahoor and Mr Naseem, the best and biggest-hearted landlords in Delhi. I'm thankful to daulat ki chaat makers Babu Ram and Rakesh Kumar who allowed me into their home in the middle of the night to watch them at work. And to the Siddique brothers who inducted me into the mysteries of kheer making. Finally, and in a league of their own, Kailash, Anita, Abhishek and Ananya Jain. As well as providing the best sugar-hit in

Old Delhi, the most sumptuous brunches at their home, and regular, delicious deliveries of their home cooking, the 'Old and Famous' family have given more help than I could possibly have wished for throughout the writing of this book.

Above all, though, I couldn't have written this book without the endless encouragement, solid gold advice and support of my husband and co-discoverer of Old Delhi, Dean. For all those pep talks while dog-walking in Lodhi Gardens, and much, much else, I am eternally grateful.